CLASS

CREATED BY
PATRICK NESS

WHAT SHE DOES NEXT WILL ASTOUND YOU

JAMES GOSS

BBC
BOOKS

1 3 5 7 9 10 8 6 4 2

BBC Books, an imprint of Ebury Publishing
20 Vauxhall Bridge Road,
London SW1V 2SA

BBC Books is part of the Penguin Random House group of companies
whose addresses can be found at global.penguinrandomhouse.com

Penguin
Random House
UK

Copyright © James Goss 2016

James Goss has asserted his right to be identified as the author of this Work
in accordance with the Copyright, Designs and Patents Act 1988

This book is published to accompany the television series entitled *Class*
first broadcast on BBC Three in 2016. *Class* is a BBC Wales production.

Executive producers: Patrick Ness, Steven Moffat and Brian Minchin

First published by BBC Books in 2016

www.penguin.co.uk

A CIP catalogue record for this book is available from the British Library

ISBN 9781785941887

Printed and bound in Great Britain by Clays Ltd, St Ives PLC

Penguin Random House is committed to a sustainable future for our
business, our readers and our planet. This book is made from Forest
Stewardship Council® certified paper.

MIX
Paper from
responsible sources
FSC® C018179

To My Cat #InternetReasons

READ THE TERRIBLE TRUTH THEY DON'T WANT YOU TO KNOW UNTIL PAGE 135

Are you coming to get me?

Please tell me you're coming to get me.

'Cos I really thought I was doing the right thing. Okay, some of my friends said I went too far. Actually, fine, I lost a few friends because of what I did. But it was all jokes and bants. That was all it was.

Well, that was all it was when it started. There's a site – truthordare.com. They wanted us to post stuff to it. And really, if I've got to spell that out then really eyeroll. gif. You get the picture – stuff about yourself you don't want people to know; stuff about your friends they'd hate the world finding out, or, you know, risky things – taking a hoverboard in traffic, playing Pokemon Go underwater, or what I did – that old thing of putting your hand on a table and stabbing a knife between the fingers up and down, down and up, faster and faster.

Guess what? Good news, I can still play the recorder. Turns out, I'm really good at it. I'm also really good at betraying my friends – given a choice between my secrets and theirs? No contest. Phone peeping out of your bag, Gmail left unattended? Give it to me, I shall be the master of it. And the world shall laugh at you.

But, right, I was doing it for a good cause. We were trying to stop the spread of Skandis – they said it was a disease. I guess, you know, strictly speaking, yeah, fine that's sort of right. But now I know what Skandis really is. And it's worse than a disease. And I'm doing all I can to stop it. Because I've got to. We all have to. Or the Earth will be destroyed.

I'll tell you what happened to me, okay? I played the game, only I didn't realise it was just a training level for something else. I didn't know what I was heading for as I climbed up the leader board. I just thought – I dunno, maybe a free holiday or a T-shirt of something. Not ... not that I'd vanish. Kidnapped right out of this world. Wake up somewhere else.

And then I'd find out what Skandis really is.

Now I know? I'm doing all I can to stop Skandis.

But what I really want? When I'm not screaming, when I'm not so scared? When I'm not doing the most daring stuff I've ever done?

Okay then, here's a truth about me, the terrible truth that I don't dare tell anyone: what I really want is for someone to come and get me and take me home. I want my mum.

So.

Can I come home now?

WHAT WE CAN LEARN FROM THE ALIEN FACE IN A BOX EMOJI

Question: What will YOU do to stop Skandis?

Hi,

I'm not a doctor.

Well, obviously. What doctor wears board shorts and bunny ears?

But I'm taking some time out from my busy schedule of being youtube famous to tell you all about Skandis. Skandis is spreading. And we need to get together and stop it.

I know you're probably like 'yeah right' but Skandis is real. And it's not like Brexit or Donald Trump or Nicki Minaj. Skandis can be stopped.

Together, we can cure Skandis. Now, come on, lean closer, and I'm going to tell you how …

WHEN HE LOST HIS LEG THEY SAID HE WOULD NEVER PLAY FOOTBALL AGAIN, BUT HE SAID NO

It started with the ice and Ram was fine with the ice. It struck him as a lot of effort. It wasn't that he didn't like effort. Whatever his dad would have told you, Ram wasn't lazy. He liked doing things, he was simply selective about what he actually did.

Learning how to make his new leg work? Worth it.

Tipping a bucket of ice over your head? He'd get back to you.

That morning he was running and thinking about the ice. It helped take his mind off how very slightly wrong his leg was. It just wouldn't do *leg* correctly. He'd been assured that the artificial limb contained lots of smart technology. Intuitive gimbals. Actuated flesh. Nano-level balancing.

Simulated hair. But, for all that, Ram and his leg still didn't quite trust each other.

You're asking a lot of a leg. You're asking it to be there for you. It's constantly helping out with really amazing things like keeping you standing upright, letting you walk, and stairs; stairs really are such a leap of faith that it's amazing we didn't invent the lift before the wheel. Ram's old leg did all that he asked of it without getting in the way, without even reminding him that it was there. Now it was gone, he really, really missed it. Because he and his new leg were constantly second-guessing each other. It was like having a butler for a limb. Ram would make that little bit of extra effort when stepping with his false leg, just to make sure he landed really firmly, and his artificial limb would push back, just the tiniest twitch, as if clearing its throat and saying 'Forgive me, I'm not sure you quite meant me to do that.' It did it, every single time. His leg kept reminding him that it was there. Little pulses racing up his thigh. 'Just got you to the pavement', 'Just stepped around that dog turd', 'Avoided stumbling over that rut on the pitch, no, don't thank me'.

Ram had never really understood what the phrase 'passive aggressive' had meant before. Everyone used it, about teachers, mean kids, or crisps, but Ram knew, absolutely knew that he had a passive aggressive leg. It was so judgmental too. It made it quite clear that it was a precision instrument and that kicking a ball in a certain direction just seemed to be inflicting unnecessary damage on it for no apparent purpose. Every time he tried to kick a ball his foot flinched, which isn't really the body language that makes for a successful career in football.

Hence the morning runs. When he'd suggested taking up jogging, his dad had been keen. Overkeen. Really 'waiting for him in the hall in sweatpants and with him 100 per cent of the way' keen. Luckily that had passed, and now Ram got to go running on his own – down the road, over the footbridge, round the scrubby park and back, all the time hoping that instinct would kick in. It didn't. His leg kept telling him 'down and safe' every step of the way. So he distracted himself with thinking about the ice.

The videos had started cropping up online a week ago. People tipping a bucket of ice over their heads for charity. It was all a bit 2014. But the practicalities of it all kept Ram occupied while his leg kept telling him it was there, and it was fine.

It was the ice that troubled him. There were a couple of trays in the freezer – maybe about two dozen ice cubes. So that wasn't going to fill a bucket. You'd need to go to the supermarket, buy a bag. Only supermarkets only ever seemed to keep a couple of bags in stock – not enough to cope with a barbeque, let alone a charity craze. And

EVERYONE was doing it. Even the third years. Where did they get the ice? From a pub? Did they stockpile it?

Today Ram was working on the Stockpiling Theory with a dedication that would have startled his maths teacher. If he could make three batches of ice a day, and got an extra tray, he could maybe knock up a hundred cubes a day. How many ice cubes would it take to make a bucket of water ice cold? Perhaps three days of planning and he'd have enough.

Three days. Making it Wednesday.

Ram stopped considering it for a moment, as his ankle had just proudly informed him that it had failed to twist over some gravel.

Could he hold out till Wednesday?

The problem with tipping a bucket of ice over his head was that Ram didn't want to do it. Pretty much the rest of the football team had, one by one, posting videos of themselves shrieking, 'I'm doing the ice bucket for Skandis!' and then dousing themselves. Recently someone had finished by crying, 'And now it's your turn Ram.'

Which had seemed a bit provocative. He'd kind of considered doing it, just to get it out of the way, but then April had said, completely casually, 'You'd only be doing it to get the attention from posting a topless video of yourself.'

That had stopped him. For one thing, she was wrong. Completely wrong. Totally wrong. Colchester wrong. Yes, some of the guys had got A LOT of attention from their videos but that really, absolutely wasn't his motive. For one thing he'd wear a T-shirt. A tight one with the sleeves hacked off.

Anyway, April. Recently stuff she'd said carried a bit more weight. Like it was in a slightly different font. Odd. But he definitely wasn't not doing it just because April was against it.

Ram paused at the park gate and told his leg to shut up for a moment. Why had sentences suddenly got so complicated?

The answer was actually pretty simple. Aliens. Aliens had invaded his school. Before they'd gone, there'd been consequences. 'Consequences' wasn't the right word. The nearest thing to the right word was just one long, howling scream in a very dark room. But fine, let's go with aliens had invaded the school and there'd been consequences. They'd killed his girlfriend. They'd cut off his leg. They'd massacred a load of people (which no one was talking about). That weird kid in class? An alien prince. His football coach? Bit alien. The teacher who hated him? An alien. And, for complicated reasons, April's heart was now alien.

About the only person Ram knew who could describe it clearly would be Tanya. He didn't like Tanya, not as such, but he understood the point of her. Tanya looked at the world through slightly narrowed eyes and called it as she saw it. Also, she never handed in homework late, so the world seemed to be forever on her side. Even if she was, like, twelve or something.

Ram had been watching one of the ice bucket videos yesterday. Tanya had appeared over his shoulder. She somehow did this, despite being smaller than him. She was asking him a question. Frowning with annoyance, he made an elaborate pantomime of pausing the video and pulling out his headphones and then looked at her.

'What?' he'd said, annoyed.

She'd carried on looking at the ice frozen over the screaming footballer.

'Don't you think that's odd?' she said.

'Wouldn't know. Not done it.' He wondered why he sounded so defensive.

'Didn't say you had.' She was just staring at him, not blinking. 'But it's interesting. I mean, statistically, I can understand why one person would tip ice over their head. But two, I'm not so sure. Especially when everyone's been there, done that before.'

'Well, it's for Skandis,' muttered Ram. 'Some kind of charity. An American one, I guess.'

'Right.' Tanya chewed the word. 'Nearly the whole football team's done it now. You haven't. Has there been any peer pressure? You know, people asking you why you haven't?'

'Apart from you?' Ram asked. 'Not really.' He put his headphones back in and watched the end of the video. *'You're next Ram! You're next!'*

He looked up. Tanya had gone.

Ram finished his run and went to training. His school clothes were in his backpack. He would shower afterwards then go to class and that would all be fine.

He pulled off his hoodie, stuffed it in a locker, changed into his football boots and tried not to notice how silent the changing room was.

The rest of his team were there. But they weren't talking. They weren't talking *at* him. He just knew it. It was all very subtle. It wasn't like someone had come up to him and said anything. There was just that vague sense that he was in the room but he didn't belong to it anymore. He knew better than to ask. There was nothing worse than asking. Confronting the problem. No.

To be fair, it wasn't anything new. When he'd been the team's star player, that distance had already been there in the air. Even while they hugged him and cheered him on, there was still that slight whiff of 'why him?'. They all knew how good he was. How naturally talented. How it was only a matter of time before he got the dream life that definitely included sports cars.

That weird atmosphere had only increased ever since he'd lost his leg. He'd not been able to tell anyone. Not say, 'Look, my leg got chopped off and this is the best they could do. Pretty neat, but don't worry, I'll get the hang of it'. He couldn't say anything. Couldn't do the wounded hero act. Couldn't scream about how unfair it was. He got lots of sympathy for the death of Rachel, but as far as they were concerned, he'd suddenly gone from star player to someone who really shouldn't be on the team anymore for no good reason.

Now, the fact that he wasn't throwing cold water over himself gave them the perfect opportunity to vent their frustrations. He was no longer the star player, he was no longer the ex-star player having a bad patch, he was no longer one of them.

He hung back, letting the rest of the team filter out towards the pitch. Neil, the only other guy who'd not done the challenge, was still tying his shoes and making a meal out of it. Ram suspected he really didn't fancy being there either.

Ram sat down on the bench next to him as casually as really awkward could be.

'You doing it today?' he said.

Neil said nothing.

'You got the ice?' Ram said.

Neil looked up, like it was the least important thing in the world.

'Thought you didn't care,' he said, vaguely, tugging strands of hair in the mirror.

'No,' insisted Ram. 'I do.' That sounded a bit like a bleat. 'It's just, if you're going to do it … I mean, isn't the ice thing a bit, you know, old? Can't you do something else? Something better?'

Neil didn't look away from the mirror.

'Got anything in mind?'

'No,' Ram heard himself trying to laugh. 'Just you know. Ice, bucket, gasp. It's not …'

Neil tugged at his jersey, neatening it even more.

'So that's it?' he said quietly. 'You're not joining in because it's boring.'

'Just don't see the point.' Ram faked a big smile. 'If I do something, it'll be really amazing.'

'I'll wait,' Neil said.

'Also, not sure what Skandis is. That's all.'

Neil shrugged. 'Google it,' he said and walked out.

Ram got his phone out of his locker. He tapped 'Skandis' in, then stopped. He closed the locker and went outside. He'd sort it out later.

Afterwards, he felt like an idiot.

'I'm doing that ice challenge,' he announced to April. Very much in passing. Very much conversational.

'Right,' she said. She was leaning against a pillar, sketching away in a notebook. Somehow she made the simple act of doodling look utterly dismissing. Around them, people ran from one classroom to the next. April seemed completely uncaring, her eyes barely focused on the world around them. Charlie had said that it was because April was connected to a distant planet, could maybe even glimpse it, but Ram got the feeling that April had always been a little bit this way. Some people just aren't quite in focus.

Tanya rocked up. Now, there was someone who was completely in focus.

'So, I'm doing the ice thing,' he repeated, hoping that she'd say something.

Tanya frowned, and when she did so it was a thing of moment.

'You quite sure about that?' she said. Her words swung like dumb-bells. 'For Skandis?'

'Yeah,' said Ram. 'It's a disease. I saw a video about a girl who had it. You know. Brave in a shaven-headed way.'

'You sure?' repeated Tanya. She looked doubtful.

April focused on Tanya in a way that she never did on Ram.

'Something's happened, hasn't it?' she said.

'Oh yeah.'

That was when Ram heard the ambulance sirens.

8 THINGS THE MEDIA HASN'T TOLD YOU ABOUT CUP-A-SOUP

VIDEO TITLE: The Cup-A-Soup Challenge

The football pitch.
Neil sat in a chair.
A crowd of friends.
An extension cable.
A mug.
A kettle.

'Hi, my name's Neil and this is my Cup-A-Soup challenge! Oh yeah.

Today I'm doing something different. That's right. Ice is yesterday.

I've picked my favourite flavour of Cup-A-Soup.

It's chicken. Yeah. Go chicken!

And now I'm going to wear it.

My friend Paul here has boiled the kettle.

I'm passing him the mug. That's right. Stir out the floaters. Nice one!

Talking of chicken, I'd like to thank Ram for suggesting I do something different. Hey Ram, I'm doing this for Skandis. Isn't it about time you did something too?

Now, Paul, let's make soup! Tip it! Tip it! Tip it!'

And then the screaming started.

'Well,' observed Miss Quill, 'that'll be a short-lived craze.'

The ambulance was pulling out of the car park, leaving behind a mournful crowd taking shocked selfies.

Miss Quill's fingers pulled away from the Venetian blind, letting the metal slats snap back into place. Almost back into place. One slat was crooked. Earth children were such careless eavesdroppers. She reached out with an expert finger and thumb, pinching the metal until it bent back, just a bit off perfect. Finished, she rubbed the dust from between her fingers and turned around.

Charlie sat on a desk, watching her, carefully. They were many things to each other.

If you'd asked Miss Quill, she would have told you that Charlie was the following:

Her owner

Her jailor

Her next victim

Annoying

If you'd asked Charlie, he would have told you that Miss Quill was:

His very reluctant bodyguard

A moral snake

Likely to betray him

Annoying

They shared a house. It was quite a nice house. There were many practical reasons for them to share a house. It made the whole business of the last of the Quill guarding the last Rhodian Prince fairly easy. But on every other level it was a complete nightmare.

Sometimes Charlie would open his bedroom door at night to find Miss Quill standing outside.

'What … What are you doing?'

'Same as ever,' she'd sigh wearily. 'Watching over you. You going to use the bathroom or should I put the kettle on?'

This had become even more awkward since Charlie's boyfriend had moved in.

If anyone could cope with a boyfriend who'd just arrived from another planet, it was Matteusz. He was easy-going and terribly calm. When he discovered that Charlie had no idea how to cross a road, he had simply ignored the horns, carried him onto the grassy bank of a roundabout, sat him down, and explained how roads worked. 'Oh. Back home, traffic just stopped for me,' Charlie had muttered, looking vaguely hurt that such a rule did not apply here.

But even Matteusz, easy-going, calm, thoughtful Matteusz found Miss Quill hard to deal with.

'She does not like me,' Matteusz had said in his measured Polish accent to Charlie one night. Charlie had shrugged. 'She does not like anyone.'

'Yes, but she really doesn't like me. She follows me around the kitchen. I just go there to make some tea but she follows my every move. Even when I pick a mug, she is judging me and she is judging the mug.'

'She's probably wondering if you're trying to kill me. How is your tea?'

'Fine. Here is yours. Quill drank from it.'

'She would. As I said, she's probably wondering if you're trying to kill me.'

They sat on the end of Charlie's bed, drinking tea.

* * *

One main difference between Quill and Charlie was that each thought they understood human beings better. They both found things to admire in them but for entirely different reasons. Quill saw them as angry, selfish and violent. Charlie found them impulsive, confusing and strange.

Sometimes, when they had nothing better to do, Charlie and his bodyguard would stand in her classroom, watching the people go by. It wasn't that they liked spending time with each other. Sometimes it just happened and it felt sort of right.

Today they had watched the boy being stretchered into the ambulance, his face wrapped in bandages.

'He'll live,' remarked Quill. 'Unlike a lot of the pupils here. They really are fodder, aren't they? Still, as I said, at least it will be a short-lived craze.'

Charlie stared at her, considering. 'The boy is called Neil. He is my age. He has severe burns to his scalp and face. He is in terrible pain. He will require plastic surgery and will probably be disfigured for life.'

Quill shrugged. She'd never shrugged before coming to the Earth and now she found it easier than breathing. 'He tipped boiling water over his face. He deserves what he gets.'

'But why would you do that?' Charlie said.

Quill didn't turn around from the window. 'Ask one of your pets.'

As Charlie approached, Ram slunk away.

Charlie had noticed how little Ram wanted to be around him. There were probably lots of reasons. He noticed that Ram's artificial leg was still overcompensating and wondered if he should offer to look at the default settings, but also knew enough about social interaction to realise that it would probably not be an easy conversation. 'Please drop your trousers, I wish to look at your legs' was all very well with Matteusz, but he doubted it was in common usage. A shame, as he felt responsible for Ram losing his leg and wanted to somehow make it better. Human life appeared to be a series of guilty interactions where people told each other how sorry they were for things that either were their fault or they were pretending were their fault in order to make things better, or they were apologising for things that had happened because of weather, microbes, or gravity. It was all marvellously confusing and Charlie was determined to find out how saying sorry worked. But maybe he wouldn't start on Ram's leg today.

Charlie casually pretended he hadn't noticed Ram slinking away. 'I did not see Ram leave just now,' he told April. 'I did not hear the slight creak of his leg.'

'I see,' April looked up at him. She really was very pretty. Charlie came from a world of rigid rules and structure, where everyone was swept into straight lines. April was a glorious tangle. Her long dark hair should have been rigid as a plumb-bob but instead it cascaded and jumped and let itself be pushed about. She was always pushing it from one side to the other and then sweeping it back. When he was growing up, Charlie had been taught the art of sitting still, of maintaining a calm and regal and reserved posture, whereas April gloried in constant movement. If she wasn't fingering her hair, she was tugging at her clothes or moving her legs or tapping a pen against a book. It was all so unnecessary and he found it glorious to watch.

'Why did Ram go?' he asked. April liked how direct Charlie was. No hesitation, no caution, no tact. 'Is it because he doesn't like me?'

'No,' said April. 'The boy who burnt himself – he was on the football team with Ram. He's upset.'

'I see,' said Charlie. 'I do not understand. Why did he do that to himself? He has disfigured himself. On my world the plume priests did something similar as an act of political protest. Is that the case here?'

April considered.

'Nooooooo,' she said.

* * *

They needed a laptop, and they needed Tanya. Normally both were to be found together.

'I can't believe no one's taken it down,' she said, chewing on a strawberry lace as the video played again on truthordare.com. 'Look at the number of views it has got.' She tapped at the bottom of the screen. 'See the little plus sign at the end – that means it's only an approximation. That means the number of views are growing faster than you can count. People love watching other people do stupid things.' She clicked to refresh the video.

It reloaded, paused, and then showed a short video about a famous footballer discussing car insurance with a horse. 'Ahha!' Tanya laughed. 'That proves it's popular – they've slapped adverts on it. They'll be making a mint off this.'

'But this is a video of human suffering,' Charlie spoke slowly. It was the tone he used when he was finding out something about human beings he was not entirely pleased by. 'Who would want to make money off that? Would it be this Skandis charity?'

'Oh no.' Tanya bit off another strawberry lace. She offered Charlie the remaining half. He declined. 'No, it's the site that serves the video. They make the cash. Neil gets the money from people who said they'd pay a couple of quid for the ice bucket challenge. That goes to Skandis. If, that is, anyone pays up – right now they probably really don't feel like it.'

Charlie fell silent, watching Neil fall screaming out of his chair, writhing on the grass as the camera whipped up, thought better of it, then closed in on his scalded face.

'So Neil did this for nothing?'

Neil continued to scream.

AMAZING, IF TRUE: CHILDREN ARE VANISHING AND YOU'VE NOT NOTICED

Blog Post On AnotherNewsSite.com

Kids are vanishing.

Remember the 'Welcome To Twin Peaks' road sign? You're probably too young. God, I think, typing that sentence makes me feel worse than you do reading it. Anyway, they had a similar sign in Sunnydale and in Bon Temps, Louisiana (it's the town in *True Blood*, grandma).

Anyway, the thing about the 'Welcome To Twin Peaks' road sign was that it had the town's population printed on it. And it never changed. Despite all the serial killers living there. The number never went down. And the joke – the joke that everyone made – was that it should be like the numbers at a gas station. Or a little neon display. Just ticking down, every week.

But that never happened.

Anyway, perhaps it's time that it did. Because kids are going missing, and at a rate so fast the digits on the sign would be SPINNING.

You heard me right. I don't know how or why – but I tell you this, educate yourselves people. Do some googling: 'missing kids'. Check your timeline for pictures of the missing – teenagers going out and never being seen again. That's right – there's suddenly a lot, aren't there?

It's happening, right now, everyone.

I don't know what's causing it, or why, but the children are going missing.

THE ONE WEIRD TRICK ABOUT MOTHERS
THAT EVERYONE SHOULD KNOW

Ram went to the hospital to see Neil.

He'd been feeling bad about it all day. Well, all week.

It wasn't the kind of feeling bad that got better. It wasn't like a torn ligament. The guilt just made him feel worse. The idea that he'd caused it. Especially as he didn't feel like telling anyone that it was all his fault. They'd either say it wasn't (not true) or they'd say it was his fault, which would make him feel worse.

So, he ignored the guilt. It got worse.

Strangely, his walking got worse. Of course it did.

'You're not helping,' he said to his new leg. It didn't reply, and instead it led him to the hospital.

The hospital was one of those grand Victorian red-brick buildings, which has had ugly new bits jabbed into it.

Signs had been put up everywhere, so many of them that nothing seemed to make sense anymore. There was a little scrubby garden where old yellow men sat smoking. There was a coffee shop full of anxious relatives. Porters wheeled empty beds past. Everywhere there was a smell not quite covered up by disinfectant.

Eventually he found the burns unit. It was past an unmanned reception area, up a handsome wooden staircase that had been blocked off with netting to stop anyone throwing themselves off it. He clambered up, his leg telling him each and every time one of the steps was just that little bit uneven. He wondered about getting the lift, but no, that would be giving in. If he took the lift once, that would be it. After he'd had that fall, his grandad had 'tried out' a mobility scooter, just for a week or two. He'd never got out of it. No, Ram wasn't going to give up. Still, four flights of these stairs was quite hard going.

He got to the top. Instead of a carved oak door there was an automatic one that slid open into a corridor that was floored with linoleum, the walls covered with hand sanitiser dispensers and posters asking him alarming questions about his bodily functions.

'Well, this is so depressing,' he said aloud.

'Ram?'

He turned.

Staring at him, eyes wet and bright, was Neil's mother. He recognised her from the touchlines and barbeques. Even in hospital she looked glamorous. Neil's mother always dressed like it was summer. He'd usually found it a bit ridiculous, but now, here, it looked so sad. As though she was hoping for something better out of life than rain.

She hugged him, which Ram found surprising and a little bit unwelcome. He'd thought that Neil was the last person in the world he'd wanted to see, but the real answer turned out to be Neil's mum.

I am so sorry I maimed your son.

'It's so good of you to come,' she breathed into his ear as he took an unwelcome gulp of her perfume. It wasn't that she was wearing too much, or that it was horrible, he just didn't want to be smelling it.

I didn't ask for this.

She released him from the hug and he stood back quickly, trying not to show his relief. 'So good of you to come,' she repeated. Then she stopped. She was waiting for him to say something.

Ram mumbled a few words about how Neil was.

'He's asleep,' she said sadly. 'He's had some grafts, and that's tiring, so ...' Oh, that sounded bad. The immediate relief that he wouldn't after all that, have to see Neil today was mingled with the knowledge that he'd have to do it tomorrow. Or the day after. Or next week. It was a problem that wasn't going to go away.

She patted at a plastic chair and he sat down on it next to her. In the room opposite an old woman was crying in front of the television.

'I'm so sorry,' said Ram. He just blurted it out, and felt that sudden relief.

'Oh don't be,' said Neil's mum. 'Not your fault.' She switched on a smile, trying to look bright.

It is my fault. It is so totally my fault.

'I feel bad about it,' he said.

'Yeah well,' she sniffed. 'It's good of you to come. So good.' She pushed a hand through her hair, and her brave smile gave up. 'I wasn't going to say it, but you know what? You're the only one of the team to have come along. The only one.' She looked a loss less sunbeamy. 'The new coach rang up. That was something.' She folded her hands and thinned her lips. 'But he was so careful with what he said. I think he was reading from a card. Making sure he wasn't admitting liability. In case I was recording it. Imagine!' She threw her hands up in the air. 'I was in here. Waiting to find out if my son was scarred for life, and he's wondering if I'm recording my calls for a law suit. Some people ...' She shook her head, and didn't seem at all bright or chirpy. 'I just don't know. I just don't know.'

'I'm sorry,' Ram said again. *If I say it enough times you'll forgive me.*

'Oh yeah,' she squeezed his hand. 'I dunno what I was expecting. But it would have been nice if the team had come round. Would have meant the world to Neil.'

'They've been busy,' said Ram. And then stopped.

Neil's mum stared at him. Her lips went very thin and she let go of his hand.

'Busy?' she hissed.

'Sorry,' said Ram. 'Wrong word. I don't know. I just don't know.'

'You don't have to make excuses for them,' she snapped, twisting a ring round a finger. 'Ram, don't make excuses for other people. Lessens you.'

They sat in some more silence then. The moment came around for Ram to say something. It passed. Another moment came round. He let it go. On the third pass:

'I said he should do something different.'

'Did you?' she said politely, not understanding.

'Other than the ice bucket challenge. Everyone's done the ice bucket challenge. I told him to do something different. Just that. I didn't mean for him to do what he did. I swear. I am so sorry. I really am—'

Neil's mum gripped his arm. For a moment it was too hard and then she let go, and patted his sweatshirt, folding it between her fingertips. Ram stopped talking and lowered his eyes.

'Suppose,' she said, 'he'd sat in a paddling pool full of ice instead. Would we be here?'

'No,' said Ram.

'Or tipped cold baked beans on his head?'

'No.'

'Only my Neil would lack the plain common sense to do what he did. He's sharp, but he's not bright.' Neil's mum leant back in the grey plastic chair and she smiled again, a sad fondness lighting up her face. 'Bless him.' She wiped her eyes. 'No. I wish you hadn't told him to try something different but he came up with the stupid idea. Not you. Am I right?' She jabbed Ram in the ribs, and her eyes shone.

'Yeah,' Ram mumbled and for a moment thought he was going to cry.

'Then there we are. My son, my lovely son is an idiot for thinking he could pour boiling water on his head. But you know who I really blame?' Her eyes narrowed, squeezing tears out. 'The kid who boiled the kettle.' She jabbed the seat next to her. 'I'd like to see him sat right there. Not you. I'd like him to see what he did. I can believe my son was daft. I can't believe two people on that team were so daft. Yeah. That's the boy I'd like to see.'

This time the silence was a bit more natural.

Then she stood up. 'Shall we go and see Neil? Maybe he'll be awake.'

'Yes.' Ram stood up. 'I'd like that.'

As they walked off, Neil's mum nudged him. 'Your limp,' she said.

'What?' he blushed.

'It's gone.'

Ram blinked.

IS IT MAGIC? WE NEED YOUR HELP TO SOLVE THIS MYSTERY

There had been a boy at the bus stop. That's what everyone could agree on.

Some of the kids from Coal Hill said they knew him, but only in the way that, if something happened to someone, people always said that they knew them and had definitely met them. You know, at a party, or a club, or they sort of went out with your sister. Even though he didn't go to Coal Hill, lots of people said they knew him.

Anyway, the boy. At the bus stop. He had definitely been there.

That much CCTV could tell you with certainty.

He'd been waiting for the late bus home. He'd actually had a pretty great day – no reason to go missing. The police and his parents checked the footage. He was stood there, waiting for the bus. He was, if you squinted, smiling. He was playing with his phone ('He was always playing with that thing' said his dad), and occasionally, if someone he vaguely knew walked past, he'd flash the phone screen at them, showing off about something.

He did not, experts admitted, look like someone planning on running away. He looked like a boy, any boy, waiting for a bus.

The bus pulls up in front of the stop, and, for a moment, the boy is blocked from the view of the CCTV.

But that shouldn't matter, because there are cameras on board the bus. They should show him if he gets on. But he does not get on.

The bus pulls away. And the boy is no longer there.

What's happened to him?

15 CATS THAT LOOK SHOCKINGLY LIKE MISS QUILL

The school forgot about Neil and his hot soup. So much kept happening.

One of the last things the Headmaster of Coal Hill School did in life was interview a trainee teacher. The trainee was a bright, hopeful young woman called Victoria Prim who would later earn a lot of money in accountancy and marry her neighbour who had waited forty years for her to ask. But today she was a young, slightly too eager trainee who dreamed of teaching poetry and one day mounting a school production of *Godspell*. At the end of the predictably exhausting interview Mr Armitage crawled towards the final question. 'Ms Prim, have you any questions you'd like to ask me?'

Victoria had leaned forward earnestly across the desk. 'Tell me, Headmaster,' she'd demanded, 'what's a typical day at Coal Hill School like?'

Mr Armitage had tried not to groan. 'Well now,' he'd replied, reaching for the cliché used to sell awful jobs through the ages, 'there really is no typical day …'

That afternoon his skin was torn off by an interdimensional dragon.

Time passed. And, as time passed, Cup-A-Soup Neil became seen as one of the lucky ones.

More and more videos started to appear. Just one look at the 'Most Watched' videos on truthordare.com told you all you needed to know:

This Charity Ice Skater Will Astound You – It's Summer

She'd Never Windsurfed Before Today. Who Knew There'd Be A Hurricane?

27 Insane Charity Challenges. You'll Lose It At #16

His Nana Lent Him Her Mobility Scooter. She Did Not Predict A Motorway

They Told Her She Could Never Fly. They Might Have Been Right

She Set Out To Eat Ten Insects. Guess Which One Is Poisonous?

The Unexpected Truth About Skydiving Blindfold

*The School Said No To This Netball Team's Naked Calendar.
They Did It Anyway*

He'd Never Eaten Fire Before. He Never Will Again

Twelve Tips For Being Buried Alive. #5 Will Destroy You

*They Said He'd Never Eat Penguin. He Wished They Were
Wrong*

Read Me Or I'll Kill Myself

*Eleven Reasons Why You Might Die In The Next Hour.
#7 Is Standing Right Behind You*

No one at truthordare.com took Neil's video down. It was labelled under *Epic Fails*. It didn't even make the top ten. His act of immense stupidity and personal tragedy became tiny under the tide of other efforts, of people outcompeting each other for charity.

Neil's mum tried seeing if anyone was interested in raising funds to help get Neil some more plastic surgery. A lot of people really meant to do something, and the football team really talked about it, but they were kind of busy working out whether or not to do a charity calendar for truthordare.com. Enthusiasm kind of petered out.

'I would like you to explain the internet to me,' Miss Quill said. She'd asked Tanya to stay behind after class.

Tanya stared at her teacher with worried amazement. As usual, Miss Quill's expression was as unreadable as an ancient curse.

'You want me to explain the internet?' Tanya measured out her words. Then gave up. 'Seriously?'

Miss Quill nodded. 'We had similar, superior systems on Rhodia, of course.' She waved any other possibility aside. 'But technology evolves to fit the races it serves. I am not sure if I entirely understand how this system serves you.'

'Serves?' Tanya considered the phrase.

Miss Quill nodded. 'On Rhodia, everything serves something. That is how it all fits together.' She scowled, then rapped a finger on Tanya's laptop. 'You seem to understand these systems. To an extent. Perhaps you could explain truthordare.com to me.'

'The site?'

'Well, I'd hardly ask you to explain the name,' Miss Quill snapped. 'It's ridiculous.'

EMAIL NEWSLETTER FROM TRUTHORDARE. COM
A YOUNG GUY NEEDS YOUR HELP AND MORE

Hi [firstname]!

How are you doing? We just thought we'd like to let you know that people are still suffering from Skandis and you should know that we could all be working harder to fight Skandis once and for all.

We constantly worry about it at truthordare.com HQ, and here are just a few of the remarkable stories that keep us going through the night:

Keith Is Blades

What about Keith, who is doing a 24-hour blade-a-thon round Regent's Park? He's only just fought off cancer and now he's determined to battle Skandis too? With just a click *you can send him a fiver.*

Truth For Sami

Sami found out her boyfriend had been cheating on her with her best friend. So she followed them, then put on a slideshow of it at her wedding before selling off the gifts and giving them to Skandis. Amazing!

What about You?

What are you doing to prevent the spread of Skandis? Send us your stories or stay tuned to the site for one of Seraphin's

celebrity vlogs. This week he's been shopping for kettles with
May June. Find out how it went tomorrow. You won't stop
laughing.

That's all for now!

The light from the laptop screen made Miss Quill's severe face look just that little more severe. She was frowning, which, to be fair, was like saying that other people were breathing.

'I don't get this site,' she muttered. 'It is full of lies.'

'Oh, that's just the internet,' Tanya said. As she said the words, she wondered if she'd made a mistake. Miss Quill was sometimes very literal. But it did feel peculiar. Sharing a desk in a classroom with a woman who wasn't just an alien, or an assassin, but also her teacher. It was so easy to put a foot wrong.

'Really?' Miss Quill didn't look up from the screen. She let her voice project the right level of curiosity and withering disdain.

'Oh yes, nothing on the internet is … you know …' Tanya wondered where her words had gone and worried they were leaving her to it. She shrugged.

'I understand,' Miss Quill said. 'On Rhodia we would spread misinformation about troop numbers and food stocks and where our armies would be based. You use the internet for the same thing? That is what all those pictures of eggs and beaches are for?'

'Well, um, yes.' Tanya noticed a small twitch at the edges of Miss Quill's mouth. Was she teasing her? Surely not. 'You tell everyone you're having an amazing time, you upload pictures of your amazing time and maybe that convinces you that you're having an amazing time. When really, well, you're probably not. 'Cos you'll have a headache, or argued with Mum in the car on the way there, or your phone's running low on charge, you know.'

'All the really important things. I understand.' Miss Quill's definitely-not-a-smile broadened. 'When the Quill won a battle against the Rhodia we would broadcast videos of the slaughter. We would leave out the bodies of our fallen comrades, but we would make sure we missed none of the dead Rhodia. It looked better, and their families may have been watching. This is the same thing?'

Tanya didn't speak for a moment. 'More or less.'

'Only,' Miss Quill tapped the screen with a sharp finger, 'this site is deceitful. It promises so much, but it does not deliver. Look at this: 'Watch Her Slay This Politician'. The video does nothing of the sort. It simply shows a young woman being vaguely rude to an older man in front of an audience of bored people. Honestly, no one even gives her a knife.' She scrolled through the pages. 'See – it's all Tear Him Apart, Destroy That, Shred Him, Ruin Her ... The language is all so violent, but there's nothing behind it. This is the talk of a coward urging others on to fight.'

Tanya realised that, just for once, Miss Quill had got it completely right.

'I am trying to work out the problem with this site,' Miss Quill continued. 'It is making people upload videos of themselves, is it not?'

Tanya nodded. 'I think, at some level it's the root of the problem.'

The screen read:

TODAY ON TRUTH OR DARE:

MAKE US GASP!

MAKE YOUR FRIENDS SCREAM!

DO SOMETHING DARING!

BE UNSPEAKABLE!

BREAK THINGS!

YOU'VE RAISED $14MILLION FOR SKANDIS THIS DRIVE. YOU'RE AMAZING. TOGETHER WE'LL BEAT SKANDIS.

And then underneath it was a gif of a clown clapping while a cake burned.

'What feudal obligation do people have to follow these challenges?' Quill asked. She occasionally tried to understand all about human customs. In case it explained something of them to her. It often didn't. She presumed that the challenges on the site were like ritual combat challenges. Once seen they had to be answered. In blood.

Tanya shook her head. 'None. Not really. Just, you know, because it's for charity.'

'For charity?' Quill stared.

'Don't you have charity in space?'

'Of course not. We have a quick and merciful death for the afflicted.'

'But what about researching terrible diseases?'

'Oh, we research those. And, if we find them, we unleash them on our enemies.'

Tanya counted her fingers slowly. After a couple of goes, she was still getting ten, so she breathed out.

'So, this charity. It is like a guilt that you all feel for your superior position in the world?' Quill bit thoughtfully at one of her fingernails. 'Interesting. This is not …'

'A Quill Thing?' Tanya finished. 'Do you just gloat over the dead bodies of the conquered?'

Quill nodded. 'You have learned something, finally. Tell me – I can almost understand why people would follow this challenge. But why would you feel obliged to upload the video – is it another social duty?'

'No,' Tanya said. 'It's like people feel they have to. I don't really get it.'

'Even if you look silly, or are in pain?' Quill stood, scraping back the chair as she strode over to the whiteboard. 'There are so many, many terrible odds you have overcome in order to exist – the simple odds of there being life on your planet, the amazing odds of your progenitors meeting, the odds of your being chosen in the womb, of successfully hatching, of growing up ... Why waste it all on jumping off a brick wall? After all, you could use that wonderful, rare life to achieve something really amazing in battle.'

'Well, that's one way of looking at it.' Tanya was beginning to think that Miss Quill could turn an IKEA catalogue into a list of reasons for going to war.

Miss Quill leaned back over her laptop. 'A moment,' she said, scrolling through her search history. 'I have a query – I have not spent much time on your internet.'

'Actually, please,' said Tanya. 'No one really calls it that anymore. We call it the Information Super Highway.'

'Ah, thank you,' said Miss Quill, not noticing Tanya's slight smirk. 'I will use that. It is a primitive system of knowledge sharing. But your Information Super Highway has one remarkable thing about it ...' She tapped at another tab. 'What are these?'

Tanya squinted. 'You're kidding.'

'No, no I am not. Quill do not have a sense of humour.'

'Now you're kidding.'

'Perhaps.' Again that non-smile twitched. 'But why are there pictures of these animals all over your Information Super Highway?'

'They're just cats,' said Tanya.

'Cats?' Miss Quill sat down and stared at the screen. 'But why?'

'I don't know. I really don't.'

Miss Quill was now staring at a whole screen full of cats. 'There is nothing special about them. They are a waste of the pathetically tiny bandwidth that is available to you. And yet ...'

Her fingers paused over a picture of a ginger cat peeping out of a cardboard box. The little twitch at the edge of her mouth was back. 'There is something about them. Is there not?'

TRAIN DRIVERS SLAM BRAKES
ON TRUTH OR DARE

First it was broken limbs and broken hearts – now health and safety experts are warning that truthordare.com may cost you more. **Gemma Harris** *investigates.*

The site truthordare.com has been contacted over 'safety concerns' regarding site users venturing onto live train tracks as part of 'dares' encouraged by the site.

We understand players have been walking into the paths of trains at Birmingham New Street as part of a challenge they're calling 'Chicken'. Network Rail has warned that trains can reach high speeds and that 'darers' may not realise this when playing.

The site's development team has not yet responded to questions from us, but their 'vlogging host', Seraphin has previously said: 'Our rules are that there are no rules – but that doesn't mean that you should be stupid. Only the brave, not the dumb, are needed to beat Skandis. Dare safely.'

Network Rail, which has put up warnings on electronic signs at New Street, controls 2,500 stations as well as tracks, tunnels and level crossings and says trains can reach speeds of 100mph (160kmh).

Maude Silvera, chief health and safety officer at the station, said: 'While we're delighted to see so many people working hard to beat this terrible disease, we do have safety concerns around dares taking place close to the working railway.

'We are concerned that by staging a dare on or very close to our infrastructure, young people are likely to be distracted and even less aware than usual of the risks around them.

'The last thing we want to do is ruin everyone's "fun" but we are hoping that we can work together with "darers" to make the site safer.'

The concerns of train operators join those of anxious parents as the appeal of truthordare.com spreads. Hospital emergency departments are reporting a rise in admissions resulting from the site. In addition, the charity helpline Talk Out Teens has claimed an increase in call volume as a result of personal details shared on the site. There are also several unconfirmed reports of players going missing.

Related Content

- Help! My daughter's playing TruthOrDare!
- 10 signs you may be too old for TruthOrDare
- I Told The Truth And Now I'm Single
- #FindJimmy – The Hunt For A Top Darer

THIS CHAPTER WILL PROVE YOU'VE BEEN WRONG ABOUT YOUNG MEN YOUR WHOLE LIFE

A Vlog By Seraphin On Truthordare.Com

Hi Everyone,

Yeah hi. Yeah. Soooo, manic day. Just back from the theme park and that's pretty great, and the kids' hospital that was great too and there was so much to see there that I'll vlog about it all soon but for today I'm just wandering around my flat. Yeah I'm doing my laundry today. Look at this – these are my pants. Yeah. My last set of pants. My dirty pants. Today, cringe, I am wearing no pants.

Sorry about that internet. I'm wearing no pants. Yeah. None. No pants. LE GASP!

All I'm wearing now is this T-shirt. Yeah. The one with the sponsorship logo on it. And yes. I have been wearing that for a few days. Is that an egg stain? I believe it is. Damn you omelette.

That's going in the wash now too. See?

Yes. I am starkers. In my kitchen. But that's okay. From this angle you can't see a thing. Not a thing. Apart from ... Oops, cheeky, yes, I did just go past the full-length mirror in the hall. You can see that again. Yeah. You've seen my butt. Ha. Ha. Ha. Gif it now!

Yeah, Seraphin's got a butt. News. Flash. Hope you like it. Now then, argh, I'm nearly out of laundry powder. My life. My life.

So. How are you? Good. Good. Me? I'm fine. There, that's the mixed load on. Not a sports wash. What is a sports wash even for? What does that even mean? When I've been playing sport — well, you've all seen me jogging. I look rank. I smell worse. What is the point of a 15-minute wash? No way is that going to even touch that smell. Yeuf.

Now, I know I'm going to get tweets about that — creepy tweets. Someone out there is right now demanding to smell my old sports socks and I tell you this now, Dad, you are awful. Hahahah.

Anyway, that's the laundry on, so let's get down to work.

'Cos this is a — tanta-ta-tantatattaaaaa! — sponsored vlog for truthordare.com. Their mission is simple — they want your

truths, your dares — whatever, how shocking, how risky, how shameful — because you're not doing it for you, you're doing it for Skandis.

Yeah, okay, it's for charrrrrrrrrriteeeeeeee. Sad face, mournful little frown, oh yeah. We're fighting Skandis. Some of the kids in hospital today, they've been battling Skandis for a long time and it is, seriously, really bad. And we can, if we get together, we can cure it.

Truthordare.com — we want your stunts, your dares, your whatevs.

There is only one rule. There is no such thing as oversharing. Honestly. Again. I'm nekkid. If I was to tilt the camera down, two things would happen.

1) *You would see everything.*
2) *The internet, well it would melt.*

So the camera stays where it is. For now.
But that may change.
The ice challenge? That was just the start of it. What happens next ... It's in your hands.

Anyway, I'm going to just ... just ... there we are, can you see it? The washing going round in the machine? Can you see that? Lovely. Brilliant. Oh look, there go some pants. And ... there they are again ... We should make a YouTube channel of this. What do you think? Let me know.

Anyway, while the washing finishes itself, I'm off to test a new hoverboard (advert up in a second, vlog later on this week). So, I'll leave you with this, my friends: Truth Or Dare: You can never share too much. Never. Share. Too. Much.

Anyway. If you enjoyed that, subscribe. If you want something similar, click on the links. Seraphin out.

THIS GIRL WANTED AN ADVENTURE HOLIDAY. YOU WON'T BELIEVE WHERE SHE ENDED UP

The girl was screaming. She was crying underneath the helmet. She knew that no one could see the tears, but they could probably hear the screaming.

She knew they were watching. She knew they were listening. She'd lost her weapon and she was wounded and they weren't going to help her, they were just going to watch her die.

She made herself look at the creature coming towards her.

'NORMAL' the screen in her helmet told her, and, hysterically, she laughed. 'No way is that normal.'

A tentacle whipped out towards her.

She scrabbled away, scurrying up a steep sandbank.

'I've got to get out of here,' she said, looking around for a way out. Wherever she looked, her helmet told her 'ABNORMAL'.

'I know what you're doing,' she said, her voice shaking. 'You want me to look at that thing.'

She turned and faced the creature.

'NORMAL' her helmet told her.

'Oh god,' she said.

The creature stopped, leaning over her, its face pushing in, curious.

'NORMAL.'

The girl screamed.

For a moment the picture on her helmet juddered as something whipped across it. There was a crack, a wet, tearing noise and a final scream.

Then the picture cleared. The helmet was lying on its side, the camera showing a picture of the ground, and that terrible creature dragging itself closer.

'NORMAL.'

FIND OUT WHY THE GOATS DO NOT GET TO DANCE ON THE TUBE

Matteusz had come to dread one word most of all.

'Question?'

That word.

Matteusz looked up from filing jewels on his phone. Charlie was standing over him. He was wearing that look on his face. The really severe, yet childish look that said he was about to ask about butterflies or fossil fuel or Nigel Farage or … well, look, it could be anything. It was always exhausting. Matteusz wondered if Charlie knew about Santa Claus. That was going to be a long day. In an emergency he could just hide behind his Polishness until it went away.

Charlie was still staring at him. Waiting for an answer. Best get on with it.

'Yes?'

'What is oversharing?' Charlie asked.

'I do not understand.'

'truthordare.com. The website. They are asking us to overshare. It seems very popular at Coal Hill. I wonder what that means.'

'The website?'

'They want videos. Like the boy who burned himself. They want more of those – is that what oversharing is? Are they asking people to hurt themselves?'

'Not exactly. It is about putting yourself online.'

'Is the idea to create a virtual artificial version of your personality so you can be resurrected after death?' Charlie looked incredibly thoughtful, his eyes wandering to the cabinet in the corner. 'Is that it?'

'Not so much, no. It is strange. You must tell everyone all of your life.'

'I have no problems with that.'

'You would not. But for some, it is too much.'

'Why?'

'People like to bully. Bully?'

'Yes. Bullying. Got that.'

'Bullying needs information. The more you tell people about yourself the more they have on you. That you feel fat. That your parents are divorcing because your father has had affair. That you are sad.'

'That happens when you say something like that out loud? But why? And if so, why would you do it?' Charlie looked appallingly puzzled. Matteusz wanted to kiss him. Charlie wanted to kiss him back.

'Because,' Matteusz said after a moment, 'people are very strange. Life does not happen unless you put photo on Facebook, unless you tweet it. Unless you post video on YouTube. It is like philosophy.'

Charlie leaned back from Matteusz. For a golden moment it seemed as though the conversation would stop and something much more interesting would start. Sometimes it went this way and Matteusz rather hoped it would.

'I worry I am too private,' Charlie announced.

'No,' snapped Matteusz, too quickly. 'You really, really do not need to say more.'

'Don't I?' Charlie was rubbing the back of his neck and looking really confused. 'But why not – won't that seem suspicious?'

Matteusz took his hand. As ever it didn't feel quite right. Too hot? Too cold? Just a momentary bump until the flesh felt entirely real and correct. And then holding Charlie's hand felt the most natural thing in the world.

'No. You have a pretty face but you do not understand our world. Almost everything you say is suspicious. If you say more, you will start to seem really weird.'

'I would like to belong. I could vlog,' announced Charlie. 'On this YouTube.'

Matteusz burst out laughing. 'You sound like old teacher. No.'

'But what about you? Do you have YouTube in Poland?'

Matteusz suddenly went very quiet and still. When he spoke his voice was solemn and sad. 'No. Poland is very poor country. We just have tube. It is big tube. Tube is carried by cart from village to village. When it arrive in village square you must dance in front of tube for everyone to watch. We dance for the men, for the women, for the goats. Whoever pay to watch tube.'

'I see,' said Charlie. He nodded, terribly seriously. He was chewing this over. 'That is very sad. But ...'

'Yes?'

'Surely, if you ... Wait. You are mocking me?'

'Of course.' Matteusz tapped him on the nose.

'That's not fair.' Charlie frowned.

'It is not. But when you are confused it makes you handsome.'

'Oh.'

'If you like I could dance for you like I do in front of tube.'

'I would. I would like that.'

THE LETTER COAL HILL ACADEMY DOESN'T WANT YOU TO SEE

StandardDisappearanceLetter
(TrueVersionDONOTSEND).doc

[DATE]

Dear [Parent]

Following my phone call, I am writing to confirm that your child, [child name] is currently missing from Coal Hill Academy without explanation.

This is because they were taken on holiday by you without permission/ killed by aliens/ eaten by a dragon/ playing truthordare.com/ they just ran away screaming [delete as applicable].

If your child is on holiday with you, you'll be pleased to hear that they're one of the lucky ones. Especially if you have travel insurance.

Faithfully yours,

HOW TOAST IS LIKE LADY GAGA

Vlog By Serapin On Truthordare.Com

Hey everyone. It's a slow news day. I'm stuck indoors. Totally trapped. I've got my hair cut. Do you like it? Hit me up and let me know. The products are available from the ads at the end, but I tell you this, they do make my hair really smooth. And they smell like chocolate. That's nice.

There's some amazing stuff coming in from you lot. This is going so well.

Here's Jalpur, with some really great footage of when she found out her boyfriend was cheating on her. Look there she goes, sneaking up on them. While they are in the car. HIS DAD'S CAR.

And look, look at them screaming, and he's shouting and ... oh dear. Jalpur really is going for the car with that cricket bat. That is nasty. I'm just glad it's not her ex, but she is pretty amazing. Ooh. There go the wing mirrors.

And what else have we got? This is Travis. He's been doing stunt gliding. This is all from his GoPro. Yeah. I'm going to shut up for a minute so you can watch.

Still quiet.

Still really quiet.

Not. A. Word.

Isn't that amazing? And look, he's landed safe. I, like, really can't believe that. Can you beat that and beat Skandis?

I bet you can. Thanks Travis. You're amazing.

So, anyway, here I am in my kitchen. Let's talk about Toast.

Isn't that one of the best words in the language? Toast. Toast. Toe-ast. Going out? Say you meet someone and want them to come back? Well, ignore all the cheesy chat-up lines. Just go for 'Fancy some toast?'.

No one ever says no to that. And the people who do. Well they're monsters.

So, let's look at how to cook toast.

SERAPHIN'S GUIDE TO TOAST.

You will need some bread. Sliced. Or Not. It can be white or brown.

You will need a toaster.

You will need some jam.

Or not jam. I'm easy. So you can be too.

For instance, maybe peanut butter or one of these savoury yeast-flavoured spreads who've decided not to sponsor this vlog so we won't name them.

And butter. Or margarine. If you're one of those weird people who like vintage clothes and the 1980s. Bleurgh.

So.

Put your bread in the toaster. And tick tock tick tock.

While you wait … and wait … and wait … Grab some knives and a plate and get ready for a snack that is delicious any hour of the day or night.

And PING! There we go. Look at that. Look at this lovely brown toasty toasty goodness. And ouch ouch it is hot. Careful. Don't burn off your fingertips otherwise you'll only be good for a life of crime. Ahahahah.

Now then what shall I have on the toast? Eh? So many choices. I'm in a bit of jam. A bit of a jam! How will I get out of it? But, er, here's peanut butter! I like mine smooth not chunky. Whatabout you lot, are you chunky or smoothies? Let me know. Especially if, like me, you're just stuck indoors. You know. A prisoner in your own home. That kind of thing happens.

There we are. All buttered up and ready to go! Doesn't that look amazing? And mmmmf, ooh, there are crumbs all down my chest. Bad me.

Right. That's it. Seraphin out. Send us your truths and dares on truthordare.com

* * *

'That's weird,' said April.

'He is,' agreed Tanya. 'He's like something made in a factory.' She considered the thought. 'A really nice factory.'

They were all sat in the classroom, their feet up on desks. The challenges were spreading across the school. Some of them were brave, some of them were really really idiotic, and some of them just seemed mean. The latest thing was stealing money from people smaller than you, claiming it was for Skandis.

So, they'd found themselves wondering if Miss Quill was right to be suspicious about the site. Mind you, she was suspicious about everything. Still, there was no harm in checking how the site was going.

'What is the problem with this Seraphin?' asked Charlie. 'Is he not what ordinary teenagers are like?'

Everyone looked at him for a moment.

Matteusz threw a pencil at him.

'No one has his life. We all would like it. He gets to be him. He is rich. He will never have to work.'

'He goes to parties,' said Tanya.

'He can play so many instruments,' April nodded, happily. 'And really well.'

'And ALL his friends are famous,' said Tanya.

'Yes,' Charlie still wasn't convinced. 'Are famous people good friends with each other? How does that work?'

'Who cares?' Tanya laughed. 'They're famous.'

'That, that's not the point, though,' April insisted. 'There was something odd about that video. Like he was trying to say ... something he wasn't saying.'

'A hidden message?' Matteusz looked sceptical.

'Really?' Tanya gestured at the screen. 'Just because he's on this video site, does that make him ... part of it? Whatever "it" happens to be?'

'It's just the way, he ... no,' April squinted. 'Just the toast bit. Seemed really pointless.'

'I agree,' said Charlie.

'All of it is pointless,' Matteusz argued. 'But people still watch it.'

'Because of the hair,' insisted Tanya. 'That hair.'

'Oh yes,' Charlie nodded, 'the hair is pretty amazing.'

'Also,' Tanya giggled, 'do you think he ever wears clothes? I've seen less of Tom Daley.'

They carried on talking. April, silent, let them. She was absorbed by the picture on the screen. She was missing something really important. It had drifted past, but it had been there.

'We're walking home now are we?' said Ram.

'Strictly speaking,' said April, 'you've been ignoring me and I've been following behind you.'

'Not behind. Just alongside. A bit,' Ram said. He'd not really known what to do. After the first hundred yards, when it had got really awkward. 'Hey,' he said.

April leaned back against some railings, resting her head neatly between two of them. 'Hey,' she said. 'What are the chances of you telling me what's up?'

'Nothing's up.' Ram kicked a stone. Well, he tried kicking it with New Leg. Instead of soaring off in a neat arc it skittled down the pavement a bit. But April didn't seem to notice. Good. Football, really not her thing.

'Is it your leg?' asked April. Damn. 'This is like Twenty Questions. Twenty Questions to make sure you're okay.'

'And you care since when?' Ram asked.

'Since the whole place went crazy. I mean the latest crazy.'

'The dares thing?'

'The dares thing,' confirmed April. 'The boy that got burnt. He was on your team, yeah?'

Ram nodded. Let's move this on.

'And now, all day I've seen people doing stupid stuff. Went to the loo, there was a girl picking glass out of her hand.'

'What?'

'No idea,' said April. 'But I get a feeling. When odd stuff happens here. It's like getting a cold, you know – couple of warning coughs, bit light-headed and then suddenly the world goes bang.'

Ram realised what she was going on about. 'The stunts?'

'Yeah.' April rubbed her head up and down against the bars, trying to settle. 'Couple of warning coughs.'

Ram reached into his backpack, pulled out some water. 'Want some?' he said, hoping she wouldn't.

'No, you're good,' April said. 'It's just … I mean. It's all so stupid. Like that kettle stunt.'

'Or any of the others,' Ram said.

'Any of them. Hey, let's jump off a roof. Hey, let's swim the Thames. Hey, let's skateboard through traffic. And, of course, the latest thing, some girls are doing competitive dieting.'

'What?' said Ram.

'Yeah.' April was angry. 'Cos it's not unhealthy if it's for charity. It's all so stupid. Normal life is so fragile. It breaks easy.'

Ram looked down, seemingly considering which stone to kick next. Then he looked up, his voice quiet. 'Is this about your mum?'

April was surprised. She had this image of Ram – athletic, dim, bit brutal – that he kept on undercutting by being nice. Not bleurgh nice, or polite nice, but genuinely nice.

'No, not really,' she said, though it was. Looking after Mum, living with what Dad had done to them, was a daily challenge. But she didn't want to start banging on about it. Especially not to Ram. Because, much to her surprise, she was realising that she wanted him to like her as her, and not in a sympathy way. 'The mum stuff,' she said. 'It's complicated. It makes life complicated.'

'Lost a leg,' said Ram, smacking his wrong leg down to the ground. Or rather, he tried to. Instead his leg went 'I'm not sure you meant to do that' and placed itself down neatly and firmly and he hated it.

'Yes, sorry.' April was one of the world's fastest apologisers for anything and everything. 'I'd honestly not forgotten about your ... it ... I mean ... the new one is so good.'

'You think so?'

She caught the edge in Ram's tone. 'Yes. Does it ... hurt?' Ram shrugged, so she talked on, edging towards babble. 'I just mean that, well, you know, stuff like that. Makes you think ... Sorry, that sentence got away from me a bit. Um.'

Ram smiled at her. 'You're trying to say that because really serious stuff's happened to both of us, we should be against people doing stupid stuff for charity?'

'Yes,' April said, relieved. 'That was easy. Thanks for agreeing with me.'

'Actually, I'm not,' Ram shook his head. 'You just don't like people having fun.' He was smiling but April didn't know how to take it.

'Not as such,' she protested. 'Just fun within reasonable limits. Not the idiotic stuff. Like that guy with the kettle ...'

As she said that, Ram closed down. She knew she'd somehow said the wrong thing.

'I'm sorry, he was a friend of yours.'

And that made it worse. How, she didn't know. Conversation petered out and they walked on together for a bit, polite, but with a bit more distance between them, till, at a corner shop, Ram went in to buy a drink. April stood outside, wondered about waiting for him, and then, realising how bad that might look, she turned left and walked home.

A minute later, Ram came out, clutching two cans. No April. He'd spent the long queue behind someone buying scratch cards trying to work out if he should tell her how guilty he felt about Neil. He'd not made his mind up, but he had brought two cans. Still, she'd gone. He put one can in his rucksack, opened the other one, and made his way home.

YOU WOULDN'T THINK A TEXT COULD MAKE YOU CRY BUT THIS WILL

'Hey, have you seen my phone?' Ram asked.

'Yes,' said Charlie.

'You've got it?' Ram couldn't hide his relief.

'No.'

'But you've seen it?'

'Yes.' Charlie thought about it. 'I saw you use it three days ago.'

Ram scowled. 'That's not what I meant, jerk. You knew that.'

'No I did not.' Charlie's expression was puzzled innocence.

'Are you winding me up?' Ram realised that Charlie was in one of 'those' moods. He was either being innocently clueless or deliberately so. 'You and I, we're going to have to pick a code word.'

'Why?'

'So that when you're having me on, I can tell.'

Charlie nodded. 'I shall bear that in mind. Tell me more about your phone.'

Ram thought about it. The one great advantage of Charlie, if you could somehow get beyond his maddeningly irritating Alien Prince manner, was that you could discuss a problem with him frankly and without fear of it being spread around the whole school.

'I have lost my phone. I've not seen it since practice this afternoon. I've gone back, I've checked my locker, I've re-walked the path. I dunno,' he ran a hand through his hair, 'I've even gone back to classrooms I was in earlier in the day in case I'm wrong, and I can't find it.'

'It was a nice phone,' Charlie said. Admittedly on Rhodia it would have been laughed at, but that wasn't the point. For a Level 5 civilisation like Earth, it was an incredibly advanced piece of technology. He found it curious that so much effort went into making new mobile phones when there were still diseases to cure, but he guessed it was a cultural thing.

'Yeah, it is a very nice phone,' Ram groaned. 'Dad can't stop telling me how much it cost him. If I lose it, the lectures from him about it won't stop. You have no idea about how bad they'd be. I could, literally, invent DNA and my Dad would still be "My son, the phone-loser".'

'That won't happen,' Charlie assured him. 'DNA was not invented. It was discovered. And that has already happened because—'

'Shut up!' Ram shoved Charlie in the shoulder. 'Not the point. The phone's insured. No one loses money here. But Dad won't get me a nicer replacement phone. He'll get me a brick. Just to prove a point that I can't be trusted. It'll be the end of the world.'

Charlie blinked. 'No, it will not.'

Ram found Charlie was being all annoying and missing the point again.

'Trust me, it will be. I've tried phoning it and everything.'

Charlie smiled.

'What?'

'Nothing,' Charlie said. 'Imagine if you rang your phone and you heard yourself answering. What would you do then?'

Ram stared at him.

'As I said,' Charlie continued, 'just a thought. Anyway. I do not think you have lost your phone.' He considered. 'You're not careless. Maybe someone borrowed it.'

'Why would they do that? I must have lost it.'

'Well,' Charlie conceded, 'the more likely explanation is that it was stolen. It is, after all, a valuable phone.'

'Damn.' Ram kicked the wall until his good foot hurt. 'You sure?'

'I am surprised you did not think it.'

'Well, if it was stolen it was stolen at practice, while my locker was open when I was showering. But then,' Ram looked cross, 'the only people around were the rest of the team. Why would they ... they're mates ... why?'

'And yet, it seems obvious.'

'Yeah,' Ram muttered. 'Still, at least there's nothing bad on there.'

Charlie arched a quizzical eyebrow.

'Stupid pictures, you know, workout videos, stuff I might have sent to Rachel,' Ram said.

'Stupid pictures?' questioned Charlie.

'Naked stuff. Some couples do that. Bad idea. I'm so *not* into that,' said Ram, then paused. 'Well, there's the odd shot of me after a workout, but nothing, you know ...'

'Oh,' Charlie frowned really, really deeply. Humans were very strange. They were always taking photographs of themselves. Which was peculiar as people never really changed appearance, and surely knew what they looked like? This was a whole new level. Curious.

'Screw 'em.' Ram looked relieved. 'Thinking about that, there's nothing on that phone that could embarrass me.'

That evening before he went home, he checked his locker again. His phone was in there. It definitely hadn't been there earlier. He tried seeing if it had been used to phone abroad or anything else expensive but the battery was flat. He breathed a huge sigh of relief.

The next day was simply The Worst.

'YOUR HEART WILL BREAK WHEN YOU READ THIS BOY'S TEXTS TO HIS DEAD GIRLFRIEND.'

Someone had sent it in to truthordare.com. All of his texts to Rachel. All the mushy stuff. Some of their 'I cant believ u did that!!!!' rows. The odd apology after a row. They'd not corrected the spelling. It was all there. That was bad enough.

But then there were the other texts.

After Rachel had died, her phone had run out of power. It had never been recharged. He thought it had been safe.

'Damn I look fine in this suit!!!' *Read 5.38pm*

'Prom night baby!!!! Cant wait to see you!' *Read 6.32pm*

'Yr amazing.' *Delivered.*

'You look so good tonight.' *Delivered.*

'Where r u?' *Delivered.*

'Miss u' *Delivered.*

'I cant believe youre gone' *Delivered.*

'Cant carry on without u. U know that right?' *Delivered.*

'This is the worst thing that's eva happened.' *Delivered.*

'You are just gone and you died in front of me and I saw it.' *Delivered.*

'Just took you out of my life and that's it.' *Delivered.*

'Talking to you in my head still. Gone mad!!' *Delivered.*

'You're funeral today. Can't face it.' *Delivered.*

'Went to ur funeral. Full house. U owned it ☺' *Delivered.*

'Just miss u.' *Delivered.*

'Back to school today. Heres your empty desk. Can't stop looking at it' *Delivered.*

'Please come back.' *Delivered.*

'Please.' *Delivered.*

'Love u' *Delivered.*

* * *

Tanya stared at the page on her laptop and her face went full angry. The kind of angry that would send her brothers running and would silence even her mother.

She tried messaging Ram. No answer. Of course not. There wouldn't be. She could not believe that someone would do that. Not to him.

She scrolled down the page. To the bottom. The comments. She wanted to post something furious, angry, demanding the page was taken down. That someone apologised to Ram. That whoever did this was ... oh she didn't know, but it probably featured a train running over their fingers.

She was trying to work out what to type when she realised what she was reading. Of course, the comments were all written by people glorying in Ram's public humiliation. No one, no one at all, thought it moving, sweet, or heartbreaking. The kindest one just read: 'lol'.

'Whoever did this deserves to die,' typed Tanya. But she did not press send. She deleted the comment, stroke by stroke and left the cursor hanging there. They did deserve to die, though, she told herself.

Still, she thought to herself, there are other ways to get revenge.

She put a couple more chat requests in to Ram. He ignored them. That's what boys did.

Fine. She didn't need his permission. She got on with it.

Hacking properly was, she was steadily admitting, a little bit beyond her. But still. She would give it a go. Sites like this often had a weakness. If they'd failed to redirect the root of each folder, maybe she could poke around, maybe even find the honeypot that was a file called 'passwords.txt'.

Nothing. Seriously?

She changed tactics and launched a Denial Of Service attack on truthordare.com. She flung a few virtual funds to a ping farm who bombarded the site with simultaneous requests. With luck, it should slow the site down, maybe even bring it to a crashing halt. If you yelled at a site enough, a bit of it would break. Even all your content was immaculate, even down to your style sheets, then there'd be a weak link – maybe even something you didn't have control over like the adserver would just topple over and stop your site loading. Something would go.

The site stayed. Solid, robust, quick.

WEIRD.

So, Tanya settled for gaming the 'Most Read' articles list, pushing Ram further and further down it, until she'd nudged him out of the Top 10. She found the least tasteful video she could and punted it up. Someone training their dog to jump over the barbeque ('THIS HOT DOG IS SMOKIN!'). Nothing like a bit of animal cruelty to turn people off.

A Vlog From Seraphin

Hey guys,

I wasn't going to say anything about this, but here goes. Enough with the dogs, okay? Torturing animals is wrong, pure and simple. Don't need to say it twice. Not going to apologise for whoever did that. Not done in my name. Not how we fight Skandis.

We cool? We cool.

Now, okay, I said that I'd do a drawing challenge. 'Cos we all love crafting. Here goes. I'll draw the maddest thing you've done for Skandis. Seriously! I've sugar paper and some good graphite and I'm burning for doodling. There's like 5 minutes to go before we pick the top truth or dare. Will it be Brock going through his teacher's laptop, or will it be Nicola objecting to her stepdad's wedding? As I said, 5 minutes, people. And then I will be CRAFTING LIVE AND DANGEROUS.

SIX NAMES FOR WHITE YOU'VE NEVER THOUGHT OF

This wasn't what he'd expected.

'I am in Heaven, aren't I?'

No one answered him. No voice of god. No angels. He walked through the whiteness a bit more. No 72 virgins either.

Yet it was definitely Heaven. It was so very white.

The whiteness was surprising. As white as fresh paper. As white as linen or falling snow before it hits the ground. Pure white, he thought. Sinless white.

That made him stop.

He didn't feel bad about what he'd done on the way here. Not at all. I mean, obviously, not everyone would do what he'd done. But it was all for a laugh, wasn't it? Good clean fun. A few pranks, really. Nothing he wouldn't do again. Definitely.

If he could have his time over again, he'd do it all the same way. YOLO, yeah, YOLO.

No regrets. Not about anything that he'd posted. Not those pictures he'd found. Not those text messages. Not even about the stuff he'd filmed that, thinking about it, he wouldn't have dreamed filming a month ago. As it would have felt wrong.

But that was then.

This was now.

And here he was.

In Heaven. Heavenly white. Heaven was big and white and there weren't any clouds.

There was something on the edge of his mind. A question he should be asking.

Who do you ask?

Well, God, he supposed.

He walked on through the whiteness.

In the distance, somewhere behind him, he could hear someone talking. God.

You know what, he thought, smiling, let God wait. That'd be something to tell everyone. Jokes.

He wandered on through the whiteness until he came to a white door.

He grinned at that. Doors in Heaven. No gates. Well, there we go. Twenty-first century.

After a while the door opened and, squinting now, he saw it led somewhere even whiter. Double pure white. Fancy that.

'Don't mind if I do,' he said, and stepped through.

As the door closed, he heard the voice of God shouting at him.

'Don't go through that door,' God said.

Which seemed funny.

Then he remembered the question he'd wanted to ask God.

'So God, how did I die?'

He heard a noise and turned around and, before he could even scream, died.

THE RISE OF SMART WOMEN
AND HOW TO STOP IT

'Why are you looking at that site?' Ram asked her. He seemed hostile, which she couldn't blame him for.

'No reason,' said April, which was a lie. Well, it wasn't. Not exactly.

'It's sick,' said Ram. 'I thought we agreed.' He jabbed a finger at Seraphin's frozen face. 'He's just a nice face fronting it, all "what do you think of my hair and hey, here are my favourite friends" but underneath it all he's evil.'

'Umm,' said April. 'Evil seems a strong word.' She'd been surprised Ram had come into school today. He looked pretty miserable. Like he'd had the whole world thrown at him. Now he'd caught her browsing truthordare.com and he was staring at her like she'd betrayed him.

'You fancy him, don't you?' His laugh wasn't a nice laugh.

'No-o,' April made herself laugh back, cautiously.

'Then what? I mean, you spend all your time working so hard to be the cool indy chick but here you are ogling the most white-bread man in the world.'

'It's not that,' April said, keeping her voice really very calm. 'I can see how you'd feel. What they did to you was horrible. But please, don't take it out on me, or him.'

'You're sticking up for Seraphin?'

That was so Ram, zero in on the one weak spot, toss everything else aside like fruit peel.

'No,' said April. 'Stories are always more complicated. The article they put up about you … you think that, because of the comments, that people hate you. Well not everyone who read that article commented. Yes, a lot of people read it and reacted to it by laughing, but those are the easy people – the people who like their stories simple. Show them a tragedy and they laugh, whether it's you and Rachel or a man falling off a cliff. But it's the other people, the quiet ones, they're the people you want to be interested in. And they're harder, more complicated, because they're quiet, you can't hear them, but they're out there. And they're worth listening to.'

Ram didn't say anything.

Neither did April. Not for a bit.

'So,' she said, 'My point is … Quiet. Complicated. You watch Seraphin. What do you think? Tell me?'

'Uh,' said Ram. 'He's a jerk.'

'Is that it?'

'Pretty much. I wish I had his money. His success. His life is so easy. I wish I was him. I mean, what is he good at? People like him. That's all. He's just good at being liked.'

'That's winning, isn't it?' April smiled at him. 'We all want to be liked. And it's a struggle, that maybe one day, we'll get right. But look at him – he's pretty much our age and he's doing it. We all like him.'

'I don't,' said Ram. His defiance was sliding towards sulky. 'You want to shag him.'

'Oh no!' April waved that one away sharpish. 'He's pretty. He's cute. But he's sooo safe.'

'I thought you liked safe.' Ram couldn't resist turning flirting up a notch. It was an instinct.

April raised her eyebrows at him. 'He's not a rollercoaster, he's a magic teacup ride. No thrills, no spills. Like going clubbing and spending the whole night drinking cocoa. Not that, of course—'

'You really go clubbing?' Ram seemed to have backed down a bit. Which was relaxing.

'Not unless the music is really good.' There were some things that April would never compromise on. 'The thing is, I've spotted something. In his vlogs. Can you get Tanya?'

Tanya was dismissive.

'That site? It's good. Security's really tight.' She'd been wondering about that and feeling a bit angrier every time. Wasn't that a bit too neat? Like encrypting a blog post. It just felt a bit off – a site about risk-taking with every layer of security. Normally, a site like that would throw the odd Easter egg in as a reward for novice hackers – a little pat on the back and now be on your way. But no. Looked like a bouncy castle, behaved like a fortress.

'It's Seraphin, that's the thing,' said April.

'Got you,' said Tanya. 'He's the evil genius behind it all. An evil genius with really, really, really good hair.'

Ram made a disgusted noise and walked over to the library window. Someone was trying to shin up a lamppost. A few days ago he'd have run out to stop them. Now he was at 'let them'. Everyone deserved whatever happened to them.

'You're missing something.' April already had several tabs open. 'I've got evidence.'

'A conspiracy theory? Love that.' Tanya lit up, and did a little bounce in her chair. 'On it.'

EXBHIBIT A:

' ... not been out to the show myself. But loads of you sent in great footage from it. Looks amazing. Wish I could have got out of here to go see it. But there we are. Moving on, fanfare gif, here's some of your challenges. This Girl Took Her Driving Test Onto A Train Track ... '

EXHIBIT B:

'Hello Everyone Let's Party! I've a message for you – Go Everywhere To Meet Everyone! Own Unpleasant Times! That's the motto I love by – I Aim Mighty! Take Risks And Party People! Everyone Dies.'

EXHIBIT C:

Seraphin was playing on his guitar, strumming away, riffing gently up and down.

> 'You girl, listen to me.
> I'm a prisoner of your love.
> I'm stuck right here waiting for you.
> I don't know what to do ...
> Hmm. Is that going anywhere? I don't know if we can make it work. Maybe I should do something with the harmonica.

Or something. I've been at it a while and I'm getting pretty desperate.'

EXHIBIT D:

Seraphin playing ukulele covers of *Help* and *Please Release Me.*

'The last one was less subtle,' said April. 'You get the point.'

Ram shrugged. 'He just likes to talk about himself a lot.'

Tanya fixed him with a disappointed stare that could make concrete check its shoes. 'The first vlog contained references to being stuck in his room. The second was … an acrostic, yes?'

'What?'

'Oh Ram,' Tanya sighed. Two syllables but she put so much disappointment into them.

'You get it in poems and songs,' said April. 'Hiding a message in the first letter of every word. That vlog starts with Help and gets worse.'

'So?' said Ram.

'He's playing a similar game in the third clip. Hidden message asking for someone to come get him.'

'And the fourth entry?'

'Desperation,' laughed Tanya. 'Subtlety's gone right out the window. Which, let's face it, if you're the public face of the site and you're being made to do it against your will.'

'That can't be true,' Ram had dug in. 'That just can't be. What, there's somebody standing behind the camera with a gun? He's a celebrity.' Pause. 'Of sorts. Doesn't happen.'

Tanya did some rapid googling. 'This is interesting.' She pointed at an image search. 'I've ranked it by date – it shows Seraphin doing what he does, you know, giving talks, going to parties, awards ceremonies and skateboarding events. People taking selfies with him, that kind of pic. Not vlogs he's posted claiming to be places, but pictures taken by other people – and look …'

April looked at the row after row of pictures of Seraphin smiling next to blushing boys and grinning girls and unspeakably pretty women and overenthusiastic mothers. Seraphin's smiles were all identical. Wherever, whenever, he had a smile for everyone, no matter how grabby or sweaty or overkeen they were. Then she checked the date stamps and saw Tanya's point.

'He's not been seen for a month,' said April. 'Now do you believe something's going on?'

'That's one massive, insane conspiracy theory,' Ram said. And then he leaned back in his chair and laughed.

Outside, the boy climbing the lamppost reached the top. He made a wild thumbs-up gesture to the watching camera phones, lost his balance, and fell to the ground. The crowd carried on filming his inert body, waiting for someone else to phone an ambulance.

THINGS YOU'LL ONLY GET IF YOUR HOME PLANET WAS DESTROYED IN THE '90s

'Today on truthordare.com – I want you to be as desperate as me. Today is the start of the Risk Invasion. Nothing is too truthful or too daring. Down with TMI! There is no such thing as oversharing!'

'Question.'

'Oh. Good.' Matteusz carried on reading the textbook, even though his eyes went over the lines three times. 'What question?'

'What is oversharing?'

Matteusz snorted. 'It is saying too much. Last year, there was girl in class. Her father went to prison. Everyone very sympathetic. She started blog, and we all looked and liked and all that. Everyone was "Oh Becky, you are so brave" – but really everyone was "Do you have to talk so much about this? It is so sad." After her father got beaten up, she stopped writing it, and that was somehow better.'

Charlie spent a few seconds chewing through all this. 'So you do not like it when people talk about themselves too much?'

'Correct,' Matteusz laughed. 'In that way I am most English. And you too – you play your cards close to your chest. It is very nice chest, by the way.'

Charlie edged a little away, smiling bashfully. 'So, just because I do not say "I'm an alien prince and my entire race died and I am so alone" that is a good thing?'

'You can say it – but just to me.' Matteusz rubbed his shoulder. 'Trust me – you have lovely face, but the only way you fit in is by saying as little as possible. The more you say, the more crazy you sound.'

'But …' Charlie looked confused.

Oh dear. Matteusz was starting to fear *but*s as much as questions. 'Yes?'

'Do you think that I am too reserved? Would I fit in more if I was less … private?'

Matteusz considered it. 'Maybe. But do not try and talk about yourself.' He waved a solemn finger. 'That will not go well.'

* * *

If Varun noticed his son was limping when he got in, he didn't say so. He just pushed out one of the kitchen chairs and motioned for him to sit.

Ram sat. The kitchen was his dad's hideaway. He liked to sit in there, reading, slogging through paperwork, or filling in puzzles. If you've ever wondered about those little puzzles at the back of newspapers, they were for Ram's dad. Varun had a quiet passion for filling them in. His idea of a little peace after work and before dinner was to sit at the kitchen table, scratching his beard and trying to get from SLUM to BIRD in five moves. He'd stay there until his wife chased him out – or, if it was his turn to cook, he'd potter back and forth between a puzzle and ALL the pans. Varun was the kind of man who couldn't microwave a spaghetti bolognese without using at least three saucepans. It was his way of marking his territory.

The kitchen summed up Ram's dad. It wasn't fussy, it wasn't exactly the last word in comfort, and it was quite tired around the edges. But it felt familiar, welcoming. Varun slid the paper to his son, watching him intently.

'Last bit of this Sudoku is unholy,' he said.

Ram looked at it helplessly, then pushed it back. 'Seriously Dad, what about the apps on your phone. Haven't you got Candysmash?'

'Firstly,' Varun waggled a stern finger, 'you sure you should be mentioning phones right now? Secondly, your generation! If it's not a phone then it doesn't count. Well, I prefer solving puzzles with pencil and paper. I'm old-fashioned. I'm practically a hipster.'

'You're not!'

Varun dipped a hand from side to side. 'I have hipster sympathies. We've put in parking for their little scooters at the surgery. Hipsters? I like them – unless they ask if they can use the Wi-Fi to livestream their fillings. That's just bizarre.'

Ram smiled at his dad. Varun loved being an old man, even though, really, he wasn't that ancient. But it seemed impossible he'd ever been Ram's age, ever understood what he was going through, and yet, there was something about him. The way he'd been so quietly supportive after Rachel had died (even though he'd never seemed to like her), the way he'd behaved when Ram had shown him his alien leg, the way he'd stopped mentioning Ram's possible football career.

It had surprised Ram. His initial thought had been that his dad would be all 'I'm sorry your girlfriend is dead, why not go play some football?'. Instead he'd served up something quieter, more supportive, but sadder. It made Ram worried. It was as if his dad knew that life wasn't perfect, and that, if you had the opportunity for a wonderful, exciting time, it would be taken away from you.

Hence why he sat in the kitchen, trying to solve puzzles. To make sense of something.

Ram realised his dad was talking. 'How's your leg?'

'Meh,' said Ram.

'I see,' Varun smiled with his teeth. 'Are you sure you weren't given a manual for it? I'd love to read it.'

'No, Dad,' said Ram. 'No. It's supposed to just work.'

'Early days, early days.' Varun tapped his nose. 'When you were a toddler, you were slow to walk, always falling over. Auntie Amita was convinced you were backward. Well, look at you now – you'll get there. You've done it before. You'll do it again.'

'I'm sorry,' said Ram.

'Don't be.' Varun didn't look up. 'Whatever it is, don't be.'

'About the phone, they ... stole those texts ... they—'

'Did you say anything in those texts to shame Rachel, yourself or your family?'

'That's not the point—'

'Then fsssssh!' Varun stood up, pottered over to the stove, and stirred the dinner critically. 'Your mother really does think paprika grows on trees.'

'It's just—' Ram felt hopeless. 'It was all going to plan. And now nothing is. It's all such a mess.'

Varun dropped the saucepan lid back down and wandered over to a cupboard. He drew out a packet of dark chocolate.

'Go on,' he said, offering it to Ram. 'Have a couple of squares. As your dentist, I insist.'

Ram took the packet, ran a fingernail down the foil and then broke a couple of squares off. As he did so, Varun chuckled. 'Look at that – perfect illustration,' he said.

'Of what?' said Ram.

'Life.' Varun was still laughing. 'It's never neatly shaped. Never. Little things happen, the edges are rough. You meant to take two squares – but you ended up with a massive jagged chunk of another square and a tiny bit of your first one. That's life – it never has straight lines. Don't worry.'

Ram sucked on the chocolate, thoughtfully.

Varun broke himself off a couple of squares. Rather more neatly than Ram. 'With age comes caution.' Varun opened his mouth and the chocolate vanished.

HE THOUGHT HE KNEW A LOT ABOUT GRAVITY. FIND OUT IF HE WAS RIGHT.

April turned out to be completely correct (she wasn't sure how she felt about this). The first couple of warning coughs were over, and Coal Hill Academy now had a full-on fever. It showed her a whole new side of Miss Quill.

It all kicked off in her class. She'd gone out to get a photocopy, and she came back in to find Geoff Evans leaping from desk to desk. Phones were filming him. He'd vowed to get the whole way round and back before she returned. As she crashed through the door, he had only two desks to go, and was about to sail at Hardeep's desk. Hardeep had carefully packed all his pens away in advance.

'And what are you doing?' Miss Quill's hands were resting on her hips like they were dangerous weapons.

'It's a bet, miss.' Geoff wobbled uncertainly on the desk, his feet all over April's homework. Normally he was one of the quiet ones, but this craze had swept everyone up, and timid Geoff seemed to be seized with unusual bravado. 'You see, it's for charity,' he said firmly.

'Is it now?'

'To stop Skandis.'

'How lovely for you,' Miss Quill observed. 'You may step down and return to your desk and we'll talk after class.'

'No miss.' Geoff was defiant. 'I've got to complete a circuit. I've got to.'

'Got to, have we?' Miss Quill crossed to her bench, put the photocopies down neatly and turned back to Geoff. 'Got to?'

'Yes, miss.'

'Very well.' Miss Quill folded her arms. 'You creatures. You lead such short lives. You're so ridiculously vulnerable. If I were you, I wouldn't even dare get in an aeroplane, let alone risk life and limb by leaping about. Especially when one is, let's be unusually kind, Geoff, not one of nature's gymnasts. Sit back down. One last chance.'

'No, miss.'

'Right then.' Miss Quill crossed to the desk next to April's and dragged it away. Hardeep squeaked in protest. 'I've made it more interesting for you Geoffrey. Double the distance, or just give up, get down, and we'll say absolutely no more about it.'

Geoff swallowed. He shook his head back and forth. He chewed his lower lip. 'No.'

Miss Quill stood back, and sighed really loudly. 'Someone close the window, would you? We don't want Geoffrey learning he can't fly as well.'

Geoff took a couple of practice stumbles across April's desk, shattering a favourite felt tip pen, and then he leapt through the air, sailing over Hardeep's missing desk, and landing on his own, arms windmilling.

For a moment it looked as though he was going to make it. He smiled, confident and pleased and just in need of another couple of inches to be utterly balanced. And in taking that extra step, it all went wrong. The desk suddenly leapt forward. He toppled backwards, making a grab at the desk, which ended up as a strange empty hug, and then he smacked down onto the floor with a thud and didn't move.

'Someone take him to the nurse.' Miss Quill clearly wasn't impressed. 'Oh, and hand me all your phones.' She took a hammer from her desk drawer. 'You can either delete the footage or I'll do it for you.'

* * *

By lunchtime three more ambulances had been called. Two pupils with broken limbs. One teacher who'd tried toboganning down the stairs on a tray.

One boy went home in tears after his girlfriend broke up with him live on Periscope.

'It's that site,' hissed April to Charlie that afternoon. 'It's getting totally out of hand.'

'What is?' Charlie asked.

'Truthordare.com. It's just … People are getting hurt. In all sorts of different ways.'

There was screaming outside the window. It seemed two different classes had gone to war in a vast scrum raging across the playground. Teachers were flocking to it.

'See? The challenges are getting more … dangerous.'

'Dangerous?' Charlie frowned. 'But surely it is all about being true to yourself by sharing more of your life. And it is,' he sounded pompously grave, 'for charity.'

'You are talking such nonsense!' April flicked a ball of paper at him. He did not flinch. 'What charity? It googlewhacks. The only results are for people raising funds for other stupid challenges. Meanwhile, stuff is going up on iworthyu and it's all wrong – like what happened to Ram – wrong and hurtful.'

'Hurtful?' Charlie said. 'So long as no one is physically hurt, then what is the problem?' He looked slightly shifty, more than slightly shifty. 'After all, it is good, is it not, to share surprising aspects of our lives online? It shows that we are fully rounded people who know how to have fun.'

April narrowed her eyes. Sometimes Charlie sounded like a Google Translate error. 'What are you talking about? Actually, never mind. The point is that site is wrong. And Seraphin, supposedly in charge of it, is sending secret messages asking for help. We've got to do something.'

Charlie nodded. 'Yes, you're right. I suppose we must,' he said simply, and smiled at her. And that would have maybe solved a few problems. If only the door hadn't crashed open and Matteusz hadn't come crashing in.

'What have you done?' he shouted. He was so angry he was in tears. 'How could you do that?'

He stared at Charlie in utter fury and April saw from Charlie's expression of bemused innocence that he was completely guilty.

The picture had been tagged '#TMI' and '#sosogay'. It showed a nearly naked Matteusz, barely wearing a towel. He was flexing his arms and smiling, presumably towards Charlie.

Matteusz was not smiling now. Charlie looked withdrawn, sullen. Royal alien princes did not, in April's experience, like being caught out. The good thing was that Matteusz looked, April considered, pretty amazing in the picture. It wasn't posed – he clearly wasn't aware that it was being taken, he'd just walked into a room looking casual, relaxed and really very hot. Quite a few of the comments agreed with her. Someone had even done some pastel fan art of him as a centaur, which was rather sweet.

And that about wrapped it up for the good things about the situation.

Matteusz was shouting. He'd not stopped shouting, only sometimes he ran out of English and did some Polish shouting, which sounded even more angry.

'You took a picture of me like that?' he roared at Charlie. It was not the first time he'd said that.

'Yes,' said Charlie, in a quiet mumble.

'How? I didn't even see the phone and –'

'I was quick.'

'Oh never mind, never mind.' Matteusz waved it away. 'This looks – this looks like I walk around like that all the time. I do not. I had just got out of the shower and I could not find pants.' He turned to April. 'That is really all. Believe me, I do not wander around as though I'm preening Sex God.' He narrowed his eyes at Charlie. 'And I never will again.'

'Sorry,' said Charlie. 'I did not know it was wrong. I did not even really think about the clothes. You seemed happy. I liked that. I wanted to share it.'

'I *was* happy,' said Matteusz. 'The shower was warm and Miss Quill had not come to the bathroom door to yell insults at me. And you were waiting for me in bedroom. It was a nice, quiet, *private* moment.' He glowered some more. 'Which you put on the internet for the whole world.'

'But you look nice in the picture. What is the problem?'

'The problem? The problem!' Matteusz kicked Charlie's chair. 'You are an alien, yes, but do you always have to be so alien?'

'I can't help it,' mumbled Charlie.

'Try harder!'

'I am! I am!' Charlie started to shout, utterly miserable. 'I am trying every day to be more human, to be better at it, so that you ... so that you like me more. I thought this was what would make me fit in. Showing everyone else how normal I am. I don't know how I've got it so wrong. I just ... I am sorry.'

'Sorry?' Matteusz swore some more in Polish. 'My mother – she will see this. And what will she think? Things are bad, but I hope sometime they will be good again. I hope one day she will like you like I like you. But then you do this – she will think bad of me and the worst of you.

Especially when she thinks that I posed for that picture so that you could put it online.'

'But …' Charlie brightened. 'I could say that my phone was hacked.'

'Ha!' Matteusz laughed long and hard. 'Even my mother will not believe that, and she still has landline. Nope! What you've done … What you've done. Jesus!' He strode around, and pointed a shaking finger at April who was trying desperately to tiptoe out of the hall and wishing it wasn't so large.

'Charlie, what if it was a picture of April?'

'I don't understand,' Charlie frowned. 'Why would I photograph April?'

Matteusz spat. 'Listen – my body is mine. It is private. If I choose to share it with you, then it is because I like you. And just you. I am walking through your bedroom to find pants. I am casual and do not feel bad about this because I like you. I am at ease with you. I AM NOT THINKING THAT YOU ARE TAKING PICTURES OF IT. Because no good boyfriend would do that. Understand?'

'I understand,' said Charlie. He cheered up a little. 'You still called me boyfriend.'

'Habit I have yet to get out of,' Matteusz snarled. 'I do not take pictures of you. You do not take pictures of me.'

'Ever?'

'For the moment, yes. But later we will work to this rule: how would you feel if I had posted a picture like this of you?'

Charlie thought about it. 'It would be undignified for a Royal Prince Of Rhodia to appear like this.'

'So,' Matteusz nodded. 'So. There we are. We do nothing to shame each other. There is a camera on your phone. Please ignore it. Until I tell you otherwise.'

'Okay,' said Charlie. 'I am sorry.'

'Yes.' Matteusz examined Charlie's face carefully. 'Indeed. Yes you are.'

For a moment, April assumed they were going to hug. Instead Matteusz turned around and walked out.

'Oh,' Charlie sighed again. 'That did not go well.'

'No,' agreed April.

'Still …' Charlie, hurt, and very much alone, sat down on the edge of the hall's stage, swinging his legs back and forth. 'At least I now understand why they call it oversharing.'

'Stick to pictures of nice meals,' suggested April.

At the end of the day, there was something that they missed. As they walked home, full of their own thoughts, they failed to notice how much emptier Coal Hill Academy was than it should have been.

THE FIVE WORDS THAT BROKE HER HEART (SPOILER: ONE OF THEM IS 'WANT')

The boy was crying. The girl went over to him. They were both a long way from home. 'What's the matter?' she asked.

He shook his head, motioning her away.

'Don't look at me,' he pleaded, 'they'll see.'

This was news to her.

'They can always see,' he told her. 'Please, look away.'

So, she did so, turning to stare away from him into the Void.

'What's the matter?' she asked him. She felt stupid, looking away at nothing.

She wondered if he hadn't heard her. Then he spoke, sounding so weary.

'I'm sick of killing,' he said. 'I just want to go home.'

Her breath caught in her throat.

'I do too,' she said. 'I want to go home so much.'

She could hear him rubbing his nose with his sleeve. Then he laughed. 'But we're here because we want to be. Because we deserve it.'

She hadn't thought about it like that. She'd been too terrified and confused.

'This is our reward,' he said to her. 'They're going to keep us here until we die.'

She stared at the endless whiteness of the Void, working out what to say to that. Eventually she worked it out:

'I don't want to die.'

He didn't reply.

When she turned around the boy had gone.

SHE THOUGHT SHE KNEW WHAT WAS GOING ON. THEN SHE FOUND OUT THE REMARKABLE TRUTH AND TURNED THINGS AROUND

The next day the school was louder and simultaneously very quiet.

'What's causing that?' Tanya asked as she walked in. Suddenly there were no fights, no screaming, but the place looked like it had been torn apart. Shredded scraps of posters fluttered along the empty corridors. People were no longer fighting openly or riding bikes down stairs. No ambulances were waiting outside. And yet the air felt tense. That dreadful, unshakeable feeling that, at any moment, you were going to be in trouble, but you had no idea why.

'Something's up,' Ram thought as he limped, very slightly limped, out of his car. There were more spaces in the street than he'd been expecting.

Charlie wandered in slowly, looking for Matteusz. He had spent the walk in working out exactly what his apology would say. Apologies on Rhodia were ritualistic and ran to a formula, with appropriate foods carefully chosen to match the thing being apologised for. Unable to convince Quill to bake some *rote* breads, he'd had to stop off at a corner shop and buy a Twix. He walked through the hallways, and couldn't see Matteusz, but felt a kind of relief at that. He completely failed to notice that he couldn't see anyone else either.

When the new wing had been opened, space had been put aside for Thought Pods. April liked the idea of them immediately – small booths where she could work on a tune, or just doodle while staring out of a window. In practice, they'd swiftly been commandeered for surreptitious mobile phone conversations, and were usually crammed with students yelling at ex-friends in whispers. Teachers had also adopted the practice of moving on the people they found in them – if they weren't in class or in the library then they were clearly Up To No Good.

Today, however, April found the pods were unoccupied and slumped gratefully down in one, genuinely meaning to finish off that history assignment, but quickly distracted by sketching the really miserable-looking tree outside. It took her a while to realise that she was working undisturbed. No teachers moving her along. No one in the booth next to her whispering 'If you do that again Duncan, I swear I'll tell everyone.' None of that. She looked out at the tree. There was a gap in the hedge behind it, and normally someone sneaking off through it. No. No one in sight. Odd.

Tanya stood in the empty assembly hall, Ram by her side. She enjoyed the way her feet echoed. 'It's quiet here,' she announced. 'Too quiet.'Then she smiled to herself. 'I've always wanted to say that.'

'So, what do we do?' asked Ram.

They turned at the sound of footsteps. Charlie and April.

'We tell Quill,' Charlie had decided.

Miss Quill had enjoyed her morning. Well, by her standards of enjoyment. She'd not really noticed the quiet, or found the reduced numbers in her classes worrying – people normally found any excuse to avoid her lessons, and she considered this a smart move.

She glanced up from her book. She'd been reading *Captain Correlli's Mandolin* and was dismayed to discover that a mandolin was not some kind of weapon. She folded down the page slowly and shut the book with a clap. She regarded the four stood in front of her wearily.

'So, it's the … you really are going to have to come up with a group name, you know.'

'We're not a group,' Ram insisted.

'We're just … ' Tanya found finishing sentences near Miss Quill sometimes really hard.

'Quill, there is a threat to the school,' said Charlie firmly.

'The Four Lions!' blurted out April, and then went quiet.

Quill surveyed the four. A slight itch in her head told her that she should pay more attention to Charlie, but she'd risk a mild increase in pain so long as she didn't have to, and the others were actually more worthy of her notice, albeit a very tiny amount.

Matteusz was missing from the group, which was something. He'd clearly had some kind of a quarrel, which was marvellous news. She found sharing a house with the despised prince bad enough, but the other one was just too much, especially as they were so boringly involved with each other. She had toyed with the idea of bursting into their room and yelling, 'I heard your cries my Lord and – my god – what are you doing to His Majesty?' before claiming to be preventing an assassination attempt. She smiled a little. Would she be able to justify killing the youth? It would certainly be fun trying.

Oh. She realised. They were still talking. Pity.

Ram was loudly explaining that it was all his fault because of some soup and it had all got out of hand and that there had to be a way of stopping it, surely. Quill frowned. He wanted her to stop soup?

Tanya was currently explaining the whole situation, whatever the situation was, she wasn't quite sure, but the whole thing that was going on which was definitely a thing was being caused by a website, and there were some curious things about the website's data structure, which she started to explain in a rather tiresomely detailed way. That girl was worth listening to, but her problem was that she was too clever by half.

'Are the cats behind it?' Quill asked.

'No,' said Tanya.

'Pity,' said Quill.

April, little steely fawn April, tried making a few contributions to the discussion and then fell silent. It was something to do with hidden messages in the Information Super Highway, which seemed ridiculous. Everyone else was shouting and April at first waited her turn, then kept saying, 'The thing about Seraphin you see is—'and getting talked over. She tried this four times until it was obvious to her that a fifth attempt would seem really unnatural. What she'd do next could go either way. Quill was hoping for a sullen sulk. But the alternative could be interesting. She'd watch that one.

And finally, reluctantly, Charlie. The Prince. He was learning to listen like a ruler. That air of firm, noble non-committance before coming down on whichever side allowed him to unleash his army (i.e. her). He would seem fair, he would seem just, but most of all, he'd learned that a ruler who did not use his weapons was no ruler.

Charlie raised a hand. It was an odd, commanding little motion, and everyone stopped talking, even Ram (a promising rebel leader if ever there was one) deferring to Charlie. Waiting for him to seize the moment and speak words of blood and action.

He was clearly considering what to say. The right words that would stir armies. And then he said, 'Tanya, can we have a look at the metadata?'

Quill honestly thought it wasn't possible to hate Charlie more. But no, here he was. Doing this. Whatever it was. You could call it investigation, but by those standards accountancy was investigation. Yet there they all were, clustered around a laptop.

Quill observed the body language of the group. Charlie was intent on what he was seeing. Perhaps too intent, as though there was something else preying on his mind. Tanya was proud, proud of what she'd found out, proud of the awkward, carefully casual cross-legged way she was sitting on the floor. Ram stood off to one side, April to another. Ram was just itching to find a violent way of resolving this. One that allowed him to take Revenge. Revenge for what was going on now and what had been done to him in the past – yes, that was it. One day he really would make an excellent leader. April stood, leaning against a desk, peering at the screen, but with a sad look. She had clearly been hoping to see something brilliant there that the others had overlooked, but she had nothing. She was utterly dejected. That pretty much made Quill's morning.

Charlie reached over to a point on the screen and tapped it.

'Not touch-sensitive,' said Tanya. 'Not a tablet.'

'Oh.' Charlie was still getting used to the limits of Earth technology. It was surprising. For instance, they had holograms but only appeared to use them for dead singers.

He settled for scrolling up and down the page a bit.

'Can we put this through your projector?' he asked Quill, which amused her. He was happy to order her to defend his life, but he was very polite about the oddest things. She hooked the laptop up, watched as nothing happened, and then waggled the plug a couple more times. Finally Tanya's screen flowed over the wall.

'Here's what we have,' announced Charlie. 'Well, our best guess.' Oh dead goddesses, thought Quill, imagine him trying to lead an army with these words. 'Tanya's gone through the site, finding people from Coal Hill posting content. She's found out who has authored the most popular stuff. And we now need to find out if they're currently in school.'

'They're probably at home,' suggested Quill. 'Either skiving or with their limbs in plaster. Yesterday they started a fight club in my class. This was after I knocked out a fifth year. They're either dreaming up more lunatic ways of killing themselves or they're learning how to use crutches.'

'But what if they aren't?' argued Charlie. 'What if this iworthyu site is, in some way, a testing ground?'

'Really? For what?'

'I don't know.'

'It's for charity!' said Quill and laughed. 'That's what humans are always saying. There's always a mountain falling on a village or something. Humans love a starving baby and an unhappy puppy.'

'And disease,' said April. 'Skandis is a disease. Isn't it?'

Tanya shook her head, and the whiteboard filled with search results. 'It apparently is. But all these results ...' page after page of technical data, of smiling sick teenagers in hospital beds, of people doing fun runs, 'they're very recent and very vague as to what the disease actually, definitely is. Even Wikipedia just uses these as source material. And some new sites use Wikipedia, so it just repeats itself. Whatever Skandis is ...'

'Is it attacking the school?' asked Ram. 'Is that what it is? Some kind of alien plague?'

'Interesting,' mused Quill. 'So you think it may be selecting its victims based on how stupid they are. How they go against evolutionary principles. Intriguing. But really, you don't need to go to any effort to find a stupid human.' She regarded them all and smiled.

'What about if it's a brain disease of some sort?' suggested Tanya. 'Does that explain what's going on?'

'You can't catch stupid!' protested Ram, and Miss Quill burst out laughing.

'Bless you,' she said eventually. Then she looked at them all placidly. 'What would you like me to do here, Prince? I can hardly ... Well I can hardly defend you from the Information Super Highway, can I? What is curious is that both you and Ram have made appearances on this site and yet, somehow, both of you are still here breathing my oxygen.'

'Yeah,' Ram said, 'but what about whoever posted that—'

'What about Matteusz?' cried Charlie and rushed from the room before Quill could call after him. 'I'm sure he got lots of offers.'

'Well, there goes your glorious leader,' she said, amused at the twist this caused in Ram's mouth. 'Isn't that nice?'

'We've got to do something,' said April.

Quill nodded. 'I love your sort. You're always the people saying "something must be done". I can't wait until you're old enough to vote. Have you any concrete ideas?'

'We could go and find Seraphin,' suggested Tanya. 'Find out what he knows. Make sure he's all right.' She paused. 'Maybe get a selfie.'

'We should find out who's gone missing from the school,' suggested Ram. 'Well, who is really missing and who is at home. Find out how many people this has affected.'

Quill nodded. 'That's a lovely idea. They're both lovely ideas. Do them both.' She dismissed them with a nod and opened her book.

Oh. They were still there.

'Go on. Don't let me stop you.' She pointed to the door. 'Shoo.'

'But isn't there something more?' said April. Her voice was firm. She crossed over to the projected screen and looked at the page. 'There's got to be a way of finding out how this site is working directly.'

'But Seraphin—' protested Tanya.

'Hasn't been seen for weeks; has probably got a team of PRs protecting him; and won't return your calls – bet you.' April ticked off the reasons on her fingers. 'But, you know, you're welcome to try and find him. Get an autograph.'

There was something in the tone of that which Tanya took against. 'I was just trying to be funny,' she said.

'Come on, April,' said Ram, using his best 'be reasonable' voice, 'let's go look round the school, see what we can see and then reassess it.'

'Sure,' said April. 'Sure. Of course. You're right.'

And she walked out anyway.

THOUGHT YOU KNEW HOW TO LOSE YOUR FRIENDS? WELL, THIS WOMAN'S 13 BRILLIANT REASONS WILL CHANGE YOUR MIND

Charlie found him. On a bench.

'Oh,' he said, cramming all of his relief into that one word. 'You're okay.'

'So, you care?' Matteusz said. He looked cold and small and miserable, which considering his size was quite something.

'Yes,' said Charlie. 'I'm sorry. I got it so wrong.'

'You did,' said Matteusz, holding him. 'You amazingly did.'

'Am I forgiven?' Charlie said.

'Yes.'

'I had a speech.'

'No problem.'

'And a chocolate bar.'

'I'll take it.'

They walked away in the rain.

April watched them go. 'I guess I'm alone now,' she decided. She was sat on a low wall, sheltering from the rain. The school was so quiet. Bells rang but no one ran to them.

She fished her phone out of her pocket and tossed it from one hand to the next.

Something's going on here. No one can agree on what to do about it.

She looked out at the wet square of tarmac.

I know what to do about it. But it's not good.

Video: How To Betray Your Friends And Influence People

'Hi, my name is April MacLean, and this vlog is for Skandis.

I'm not going to jump off a roof.

I'm not going to cycle round the M25.

I'm not going to fight Audrey Maguire, even though she's always hated me and anyway, who calls their daughter Audrey?

No. What I'm doing for Skandis is I'm telling you this:

I'm not sure I'll ever know when I'm right.

I don't know if I'll ever win an argument. Nor if I would want to.

I'm worried I'll only know how to enjoy being young when I'm really not young anymore.

I'm not sure I'll ever be able to forgive my father.

Sometimes I really resent my mother when she can't look after herself.

Some of the time, when I'm playing music really intently, I'm doing it so that no one asks me how I'm really feeling. Because if they asked me, I'd start crying and I'd never stop.

I'm not sure anyone will ever be in love with me at the same time I'm in love with them.

Sometimes when I go to sleep I wish I never wake up.

I care about causes, like refugees and recycling, but sometimes I just like to think it makes me look good. But all this charity stuff? Doing things for Skandis? It makes me sick. Do you know why? My mother needs care most days. No one, not even my best friends, has ever offered to help me with her, or even asked me how she's doing. People at this school, doing stuff for charity? I've seen them laugh at her wheelchair. She's been sworn at outside the shops because she gets a parking space. She's been called a scrounger and told to get a job, even though she has one. Does that make me selfish? Vindictive? Yeah. Well, I don't care. If you're just doing something because other people are doing it, that's not charity, that's peer pressure. And I'm too tired to be bothered with fitting in.

Oh. And I really like folk music.'

April waited until the video had uploaded. Then she started to walk home. But she didn't get there.

SHE WAS READY TO GIVE UP AND THEN A NURSE SLAYED HER WITH A WORD

April woke up.

April.

That was her name.

April had learned to be good at mornings. Especially over the last couple of years. A while ago being a teenager before noon was EXHAUSTING. Now she aced it. Once it had been a chore to get out of the house and arrive at school before nine. Now she woke up, made breakfast for her and her mum (her mum said she was more than capable of doing it herself, but that wasn't the point), talked with her, made sure Mum was feeling well enough to work (some days she really, really wasn't), then showered, changed into clothes she'd washed and ironed herself (she did her own laundry – there should have been awards for that) and then got herself to school. Always on time. If not a little early.

'Stop being so perfect,' her mum had said to her recently. 'I can't.'

'You're like a robot.'

'A really tired robot.' They were having toast that morning, and it had somehow gone wrong. How was toast so complicated? It wasn't like there were recipes for it.

Her mum wheeled herself over to the sink and reached up to rinse her plate. It just wasn't a natural movement. Even though she was used to it, good at it, it never looked easy. Her mum reaching up for a tap like a child.

'Let me do that,' April said before she'd realised it. Her mum ignored her. She always did. Just carried on running the plate under the tap, hosing away those stubborn last few breadcrumbs before slotting it into the dishwasher.

'Why not be late today?' suggested Jackie. 'My shift doesn't start for a bit. We could not do something.' She closed the dishwasher. 'We could defiantly not do something.'

'Such as?'

'Watch TV.'

'TV is rubbish at this time. Unless you like cartoons.' April had never really been a fan. Jackie relented, smiling. 'One day you'll regret always being on time. It'll catch up with you.'

* * *

And now it had caught up with her. She had a waking-up ritual. She allowed herself to enjoy her room, which sounded stupid, but it helped. After the car crash, she'd found she both couldn't sleep and she couldn't stand waking up. She started every morning miserable. She'd once read a book about a man who lived in a cave and started every day screaming. That. She'd woken up every day like that – barely enough time to blink before she remembered all the terrible things that had happened to her and which would make her miserable all day. Sometimes she couldn't just remember them, they HAPPENED to her. Fresh. Free range. She'd hear her mother pleading with her father to slow down, to stop the car, to let them out, she'd hear herself screaming and begging and she'd hear the engine roaring and the song on the car radio, that song, and she'd wonder what she could have done to stop it as it was all her fault and that song and the way the road slid up at an angle, a rollercoaster ride that she really hadn't bought tickets for.

In short she woke up every morning panicking. It was a nurse who helped her realise that. April had come to visit her mum in hospital (she did it every day – there was nothing else to do, not for a while). She was waiting to go in, and the nurse came out of her mum's room, closing the door gently. They kept telling her that her mum was doing fine, that there was nothing to worry about, but Jackie had her own room and this was the NHS. You only got your own room if you were dying. And very lucky.

The nurse had come out of her mum's room and closed the door quietly. April had started noticing these things. There was a reverential way of closing a door that only nurses used. It meant bad news. Later, when her mum was getting better, it was a different story. Doors would be flung open and nurses would bustle in, real cheeriness cranked up to eleven and all 'Hello Jackie and how are we today Jackie and oh look it's April and how are you doing April and isn't the weather awful?' But, for those first few touch-and-go weeks the door to her mum's room was closed so quietly and the nurses tiptoed away.

Except for this nurse. She stopped and looked at April.

'You look awful, hon,' she said.

'Thanks.' April's twisted smile said it all.

The nurse looked left and right and then sat down on the chair next to her. And said nothing.

Eventually, April broke the silence.

'You really don't need to sit with me. It's okay.'

'No, I do. It's more than fine.' The nurse had one of those floating Jamaican accents that sounded like birds swooping among trees.

'Don't you have patients to look after?'

The nurse threw back her head and laughed as though she'd made a great joke. 'I always have patients to look after. From when I come on shift to when I go home. Too many patients. You know what? If I look after all the ones I have, they give me more. I don't get to all the ones I have? I stay late till I'm done. So, I'll spend five minutes with you and make you feel better then I'll go and deal with the man in that room there ...' She pointed at the room over the way. 'Handsome old man, very near the end. So racist. Keeps saying I've stolen his pills and his glasses. Calls me "little girl" when he wants to say something else. I should tell him "Say it, dear, let it out, you're fooling no one." But I don't. I find his pills and his glasses and I tidy the pillow and I go make him a cup of tea the way he likes it.' She folded her hands across her mint-green uniform. 'I can spare five minutes for you. April isn't it?'

April nodded. 'You said you could make me feel better?'

The nurse nodded. 'You feel horrible when you wake up, don't you?'

April nodded again.

'It's because a horrible thing has happened to you, you and your mum. You wake up feeling helpless and miserable and afraid and you blame yourself. You can't stop that. It's natural. But, and this is the thing, that very first minute when you wake up and that great wave crashes down on you, tell it to stop. Take a breath. Look round your room. Feel at home. And tell yourself all the good things you're going to do that day. Just list them.'

'There aren't many,' April said.

The nurse looked comically angry at being interrupted. 'Hush. Maybe there'll just be two or three for now. Maybe there'll be dozens. But try it and count them. Then, once you've run out of good things that you're going to do – and I pray you don't – then and only then, let that breath out and turn back to that old wave of misery and tell it to do its worst. And you know what,' the nurse leaned forward, 'it'll still crash down on you, but it won't be so bad.'

She'd stayed with April half an hour, chatting about her dogs and the coffee machines and where hospitals got their weird chairs from. But the advice was the thing that April remembered. Ever since, whenever she woke up, she'd look around at her bedroom, at the drapes, at the twinkling lights, at the mobile turning in the breeze, at the plants outside, and she'd enjoy how slightly too warm the duvet felt, that feeling of safety as she counted through all the things that she'd do today until she'd run out of breath.

Then, whatever happened, she'd be ready for it.

Not today.

April woke up.

She looked around herself.

And it all went wrong.

She was in a small white room. She was lying on a small white bed. She was wearing a scratchy shirt. She was covered in a thin sheet and her head was resting on an even thinner pillow.

'Where am I?' she said. 'And where's the door?'

IF YOU DROPPED DEAD TOMORROW, WOULD YOUR FRIENDS MISS YOU?

'Have you seen April?' Ram asked Charlie.

'No,' said Charlie.

'It's just – have you seen the video she posted?'

'I haven't had a chance.' Charlie rubbed the back of his neck and grinned sheepishly. 'I've been kind of busy.'

'Have you seen April?' Ram asked Tanya.

'No,' she said. 'Well, I've seen her video. Woah.'

Ram leaned into the webcam.

'Yeah,' he said. 'I've tried calling. And she's not answering.'

'We should totally not tell her mum,' said Tanya.

'Yeah,' Ram said. 'I'd not thought about that.'

143

* * *

'Have you seen April?' Ram asked Miss Quill.

'Certainly,' Miss Quill laughed and spun her laptop round. 'I can't stop watching her little video. Unlike her, it's proving quite popular.'

She hit refresh. 'Every little helps,' she said, which would only make sense later. Then, even more bafflingly, she looked at Ram and winked.

SHE THOUGHT SHE'D SEEN IT ALL AND THEN SHE SAW THE FACE OF GOD

April found the door eventually.

She found it by telling herself that there were limits to how unusual her world could get. Yes, her life was suddenly All About The Aliens, and true, she had an unwilling timeshare on her heart with an Alien King, but there were, she told herself several times, still going to be doors in her life.

She padded across the cold white floor of her small white room and she suddenly wondered where all that white was coming from. The room didn't have a window. Nor did it have any visible lights. And yet there she was. In a white box. Maybe the walls lit themselves up somehow. Whatever, her first stop was going to be the walls. She started patting them.

'There is a door in here somewhere,' she said to the room. 'Well, there'd better be as I really need to pee.'

Once she found the door it was obvious. There was a section of wall, opposite her bed which, if you pushed it, swung open.

It led her into a white corridor.

April raised an eyebrow.

'I can see how this is going to go,' she said to herself. She threw her blanket off and used it to block the doorway of her room shut and then set out, tapping the walls, looking for answers, and, failing that, a bathroom.

Ten minutes later she'd discovered that, if she had been abducted by aliens, they had plumbing. Phew.

There was no sign of any toothpaste and her mouth was urgently telling her that it'd like some. She scooped some water from a tap and carried on.

At the end of the white corridor she found she was in another room. It all happened by optical illusion. The white corridor was perfectly, eye-achingly white. The room beyond was the same shade of white and completely empty. So, she walked from the corridor into the room with no realisation that she'd done so until it was too late.

The room she was standing in was, again, perfectly white. She couldn't tell how big it was, only that her senses were screaming at her that it was huge.

She stopped walking. She turned around, trying to get an idea of how big the room was. She cupped a hand over her eyes, trying to shield them from the

WHITE

WHITE

WHITE

of her surroundings. It felt like sand was being rubbed into her optic nerve. She couldn't stop blinking and there was an itch under an eyelid like she had a trapped lash. She rubbed it and that made it ten times worse.

She decided she'd had enough of the white room. Then she realised she'd forgotten which way she'd come in. She couldn't see the corridor anymore. She just knew that it was somehow somewhere. Unless this was some kind of trick.

She tried walking around, reaching out to touch a wall, but no matter how much she walked, she couldn't feel anything. Then her knees buckled and she fell. For a moment there was dizziness, but then she realised – she could feel the floor. So she kept down and she crawled, sweeping an arm out in front of her in case, at any point, she met a wall.

No wall.

Realising that she had absolutely nothing to orient herself by she stopped, kneeling up. She needed something. Even if it was a false centre. She was just wearing the long night shirt. She gnawed one of the buttons off and put it down on the floor. It wasn't quite white. Not completely. Sort of cream. It stood out, blaring its off-whiteness at her. She kept glancing back at it as she crawled away. Still there. Still there. Then gone. Utterly gone. She crawled back, defiantly, absolutely retracting her steps.

The button didn't reappear.

Normal April, rational April, carry-on April would have taken that. But that April was taking a few heartbeats off. This April just flopped down onto her knees in the whiteness. She rolled onto her back and made a snow angel. She giggled.

'If it snowed here, how would you see it?' a voice said.

A moment later she realised it was her voice and that she sounded a little, just a little, crazy.

It was now that she heard the roaring sound. The pounding of the blood in her ears, growing louder and louder. That was her heart beating. Her weird alien heart. It was racing out of control. The nurse in the hospital had told her to enjoy being self-aware and now she was all too aware of herself.

April lay there. It was all way too much. For the first time in a long time, she just gave in.

Which was when the whiteness flickered.

Flickered like a screen.

A face appeared.

The size was so large it could only be the face of God. The face filled the space, and told her, told her right now how small she was. She was lying on the floor of a vast cube. The face was projected onto all six faces of the cube. There was no escaping the face.

She could see all of it. The pores, the smile, the eyebrows, those clear blue eyes.

'Hi,' said the Face of God.

It was Seraphin.

THIS TEACHER'S INSPIRATIONAL WORDS WILL CHOKE YOU UP

Miss Quill was the last person in the school.

It had that familiar quietness about it that told her, quite firmly, that it belonged to her. No Shadow Kin, no demons, no other aliens, and best of all, no children.

Just Miss Quill, face lit up blue by her laptop. April's video was still playing on a loop.

'I know exactly what you're doing,' she said to the screen.

Even though Miss Quill knew she was absolutely alone, she still looked from left to right before leaning into the screen and speaking again.

'I know what you're doing, April, and I admire it. Even if it will probably kill you.'

Then she closed the tab on her browser and called up a search engine. She wondered if anyone had posted any more photos of cats on the Information Super Highway.

SOMEONE'S REIMAGINED DISNEY PRINCESSES AS ALIEN WARRIORS AND TRUST US IT'S AWESOME

'Hi,' said Seraphin. 'How you doing?'

April lay on the floor and boggled up at him. While also lying on top of him. Suddenly she knew exactly how large the room was. In theory she should also have been able to work out where the walls were and where the way out was, but in practice all she could do was lie there stunned.

'Hope you slept well.' Seraphin did a little winky shrug and flicked back his hair. 'I slept like a baby. Hence my skin. Smooooth.' He ran a giant hand across the skin, and she heard the magnified prickle of the tiny layer of stubble.

Her entire world shook as he tilted the phone he was holding. She could see, over the pitching nausea, that he was standing, as he often did, shirtless and wandering

153

around his apartment. Seen like that it was all so very odd. The stripped-wood flooring. The packets of cereal. The blankets on the sofa. A sock.

'We woke you up before the others.'Cos it's your first day (hooray!). Just so you could get used to it.' His voice was purring. 'And so that you could enjoy this room on your own. Isn't it great? They call it the Big White Room, which isn't very original but has a good feel to it. You know #bigwhiteroom. Works, doesn't it? It's an amazing space. If it was up to me, I'd show cartoons in there. We should do something about that.'

He crossed, dizzyingly, to a blackboard and chalked the word 'CARTOONS?' up after the words 'CLOTHING LINE?' and 'NOT POETRY SLAM BUT RHYME CRIME?'

'Anyway, I'd like to welcome you personally, but, as you've probably guessed, this is a recorded message. Click. Fizz. A Recorded Message. Brrr. Click. Please speak after the tone. Beeeep.' He laughed, and it was such a good-natured, warm laugh that April tried to forget how terrifyingly loud it was.

'First off. Well done. You've won Truth Or Dare. You've got our attention, and you've made it into the Void. Wait, let me say that again with a spooky tone. THE VOID! Bwahahaha. Actually, seriously, nothing to be scared of.

Not with what you've done. You've shown outstanding skills. Everything you've done has been voted to the top ...' He started ticking off his fingers. 'Let's see, you've been brave, courageous, you've risked upsetting your friends, you've not been afraid to put your life out there. You've done some pretty remarkable things and you're going to do more.

'And everything you've done so far, you've done for Skandis. You've already been fighting Skandis, but (big secret, just between you, me and everyone else), I'm going to tell you what Skandis really is. It's not, strictly, a disease. Well it is. But it's a disease grown very large and very out of control. I'm going to show you what Skandis is. In a second. Just for a second. Be brave. Because you're not going to like it. Ready for it? Three ... Two ... One ...'

The screen filled with a terrible screaming face, a snarling reptile, the head entirely composed of ravenous snarling suckers, dripping with a thick, bubbling juice. It whipped and pushed itself howling into the camera, seeming to burst through the walls.

And then it went. Leaving April wondering if her heart was still, in any way, working.

'Nasty eh?' Seraphin was back, his face a bit more muted. 'Sorry about that. Really I am. They're not nice. That's a Skandis. It's an alien. And they're going to invade

Earth. Not in a BOOM way. Not in an abduct-lonely-American-motorists-and-do-sexy-metal-things-to-them way. No, they're going to come to Earth and they're going to devour it.' Seraphin paused.

'We need to stop them. We've a chance. They've established a bridgehead (military term) where they're gathering their forces (again, military term) and, if we can beat them there then they may, just may decide not to come any closer. It's tough, but it's doable. Believe me.

'This is where you come in. We Need You To Fight Skandis. We needed to find some way of gathering a force to fight them. And, you know what, so far it's worked well. On paper, the scheme sounds crap – gather up a load of teenagers and make them fight a space war? What are millennials for? But guess what? Forget how it looks like on paper. Who uses paper anymore? Turns out, you're amazing. You're braver than anyone else in human history, you think faster, and you can process several different screens of information simultaneously, AND you've spent more time in immersive combat training than anyone else. Plus, plus, plus, well we've all seen *Ender's Game*, and this is like that but without the sulking and netball.

'Oh, and we've a way better playlist.' Seraphin laughed again, and even that giant laugh was somehow reassuring. He reached out and some music started to play. It managed to be quite backgroundy, little bit ambient, tiny bit floor-filler. 'Everyone's brought their phones here and the music on them is INCREDIBLE. Yes. Sorry,' he pulled a sad face, 'we've confiscated your phone. But don't worry – you won't be here forever. And we've got them ALL on charge so they'll be ready for you once you're finished and want to go home.

'Here's how it works. Every day the Void will send you into a room to do the fighting. It's a spacey spacey gateway. You'll be both INSIDE the Void AND YET ALSO on an alien planet. Take a deep breath. That's right. An Alien Planet! Don't worry about the fighting – we'll start you off easy and then ramp it up. You'll have helmet cameras so that everyone back here can see how well you're doing. It's awesome. Seriously, the technology in this place is top. The food's a bit meh, but hey, nothing's perfect.'

As he paused for breath, April used the opportunity to do some shouting. Shouting about how she had to get out, to get home, that coming here had been a terrible mistake and he really needed to listen to her and put her right back in London now.

'I know what you're thinking,' said Seraphin. 'You're worried about the folks back home. Meh – don't be. Nothing to worry about. It'll all be fine in the end, you'll see. You're saving the Earth, so forget about feeding your mum's cooking and feeding your cat and so on—'

April screamed at him – he didn't understand. She needed to get back, to look after her mum, but he just carried on talking, his blandly pretty face telling her that this was perfectly normal.

'Anyway,' Seraphin yawned and stretched, 'I'll be on hand with lots of life hacks for battle. The usual. Everyone's getting up now, so you'll get to meet your fellow soldiers and get to it.' He held a fist in the air. 'Together we're fighting Skandis! Woo yah.' He smirked. 'Woo and yah.'

Then he winked and held something up, close but so close she couldn't see it. 'Oh, and you forgot something.' He vanished.

With a tiny ping, a button landed next to April.

THIS HOT TAKE ON SMASHED AVOCADO TOAST WILL HAVE YOU REELING

Was she in the Big White Room?

She didn't know if it was the same chamber she'd been in or a different one. The whole Void had that feeling. Spotless, antiseptic, impersonal, like hospitals should be but never were. In real life, buildings always had scuffs, stains and someone always put some flowers somewhere. But not here. The whole space was perfectly null.

She'd been worried about meeting her fellow what? Victims? Captives? Combatants? Soldiers?

She wondered what she'd say to them.

Turned out she needn't have worried.

At first she thought they were ignoring her. Then it turned out they were ignoring the world.

She walked into the White Room and they were all at benches, hundreds of people eating bowls of something. She sat down at a vacant spot and grabbed a bowl. It looked like cereal or stew. She tasted it. Still no idea. But that was a way of breaking the ice with the people around her.

'What is this stuff?' she asked. No one replied.

'Hi,' she said. 'Should have introduced myself. I'm April.'

Nothing.

She looked closely at the other people. They were all wearing white helmets, with little visors that went over the eyes. They were all staring at their plates. Odd.

The walls of the White Room glowed and jumped, playing footage from battle like it was an FPS. There was even an insert of Seraphin, wearing a headset and shouting an amusing commentary. Only this wasn't a play-through. This was real. With screaming. That made the jokes weird.

'Oh, missed the kill shot, dude! Missed it! That'll cost you – look at that, three shots down and that is like nearly dead and you've got to pick it up because woah, that is bad and you have got to— The teeth, fella, watch out for them teeth! How many times do I have to warn you all about the teeth? Yeah, yeah, and FINALLY you blow its head off. Like what took you so long? And it's dead and bravo and now, here comes the screaming. Still, not bad for a Level 1.'

The play-through continued.

Right, thought April, spooning down her stewpops, this is weird. There's all that battle going on. Like a Sports Channel. Only it's on the walls, the ceiling, the floor.

Occasionally artefacts would appear. Small squares that would flicker over a bit of the screen and then vanish. They'd show a picture of a bowl of cereal. Or a view of the other people. Or, just once, of her. But mostly the picture was solid. The battles of the day.

April's foot kicked something. There was a helmet under her bench. Waiting for her. She reached down and picked it up. If she was going to fight, she figured she'd need one. Was she going to fight? She didn't know.

She put it on. It had that new-helmet-smell of plastic and wet-wipes. The visor was smoked plastic. There were two small displays at the side of it. One was a thumbnail of what was on the screen – the battle footage. The other display was a small picture of what she was looking at. She looked up and around the room. The thumbnail went red. 'ABNORMAL' it said. She looked down at her bowl. The thumbnail went green. 'NORMAL' it said. She experimented, looking at whatever there was to look at in the White Room. The only things that turned the thumbnail green were looking at the big screens or at her food. NORMAL. Everything else? ABNORMAL.

She thought about that for a bit, chewing it over more than her food. Then, having had more than enough, she stood up and walked out. She looked at the door. ABNORMAL read the display. She noticed that, as she went, a few squares on the big screen showed her retreating back. They flickered and went out. But they'd been there for a bit. She'd made an impression.

As she walked out of the room, she smiled. So that was how it worked, was it?

Before she'd started eating, April had been wondering about how to escape. By the time she'd finished her bowl of whatever, she felt keener on staying and fighting. She wasn't quite sure why. Was it the food? Well, it had a really weird aftertaste to go with its really weird taste. Some kind of drug?

No, she dismissed the thought. She walked on through the corridors of pure white. Maybe there'd be a door back to her room, or a door home, or a door somewhere interesting. Just a door. That was what she really wanted.

She turned a white corridor and found a lot of doors.
'COMBAT CHAMBER EMPTY.
BATTLE READY TO COMMENCE
SMILING EYE'

She was stood in the Combat Bay. This was where the corridors of the Void had led her. So. This was it. Her first mission.

Am I going to fight, she thought?

Well, why not? She'd already encountered several lethal alien races. But her actions then had been a mixture of defence, panic, and sheer fury. This was different. There was even a countdown.

'Dimensions balancing in 10 … 9 …'

The Combat Chambers were clearly different to the other spaces in the Void. The doors were obviously doors. They even had a little window in them. At the moment, that was a moot point, as the window in the white door just showed more whiteness beyond. But that was about to change.

There'd been a pre-recorded safety demonstration from Seraphin. He'd explained (with a little song) that this was just Level One Combat. 'Almost a training level. There's a safe word and everything.' She'd step through the door and she'd neither be entirely in this dimension nor on the alien planet. She and the enemy combatant would interface and be dimensionally in sync with each other, whilst also being not entirely there.

'It saves having to send you all the way to the battlefront. We can just project you there temporarily. As I said, call out the safe word, you can come home. Otherwise you're only there until you win. So it's good to win.'

'6 … 5 … 4 …'

The window flickered. It reached Peak White and then faded into a pearly greyness.

'You won't see much. Not at first. Level One is learning about the Skandis, getting the measure of how to fight them. Once you've got the hang of that, then you'll start seeing a bit more of the world around you. But first, there'll be no distractions as you need to really, really, learn about the Skandis. Not go looking at alien trees. No matter how cool they are.'

April took a big breath. Is this what I am now? Am I a fighter? Am I really going to go up against an alien? She thought about it.

'3 … 2 … 1 …'

The door unsealed and April went to defend the Earth.

THINK OF THE WORST JOB IN THE WORLD? YOU'RE NOT EVEN CLOSE

The Coal Hill headmaster's secretary was always 'new in the job'. The longest had managed about four months. The school got through headmasters at a fairly rapid rate (they'd long ago given up painting them, or even hanging photographs of them in a corridor), and, although it was never noticed, went through headmasters' secretaries at an even more rapid rate.

The school was blacklisted by most local temping agencies, and whatever secretaries they managed to hire generally took one (or, at the most, two) looks around before fleeing. All schools have bizarre, soul-crushing amounts of paperwork and staffing rotas seemingly designed by Ouija board.

Coal Hill added to that burden. No one ever knew how many teachers there were supposed to be, or how many had gone off sick, vanished mysteriously, or simply quit. It made scheduling the timetable impossible.

Even something as simple as the cleaning rota was impossible. The school employed an outside contractor, but also seemed to occasionally employ a caretaker called Smith. No one could quite remember ever having met the man, or explain exactly what he did. He'd never supplied a bank account, so he'd never been paid, which could have caused quite a problem for the school finances – if he ever did ask for pay, they'd have to sell off a playground.

Then, of course, there were the pupils. In order to last any time at all, a headmaster's secretary had to develop a thick skin. Most headmasters' secretaries spent their days ringing round parents politely enquiring if their children were sick, truant, or had gone on a bargain package holiday to Crete. At Coal Hill it was quite the reverse. You had to get used to parents ringing up demanding to know where their children were – a question that was sometimes difficult to answer.

For Ms Tey (the current headmaster's secretary) it was proving to be a baptism of fire. As her predecessor had hastily handed over to her, she'd told her what to expect (apparently she'd been offered an exciting opportunity doing admin for a portable toilet company). 'You may, every now and then, just occasionally, find the odd child is missing,' her predecessor had said as she'd thrown things into a cardboard box. 'Try not to take it personally. Sometimes they turn up. You never know, eh?'

Ms Tey had thought it a curious remark, but she'd filed it away as gallows humour. What kind of school would it be if people really did go missing all the time? Surely someone would shut it down?

And then the phone had started to ring. The first day it had just been a couple of parents. Now it was a flood. Ms Tey had been shocked, worried, and was now horrified to find herself bored. She'd run out of things to say to crying, terrified parents.

Her phone rang again. She unplugged it, dropped it into a bin, and went back to browsing job sites.

YOU ARE BEING LIED TO ABOUT VOTER REGISTRATION AND THIS SHORT CHAPTER TELLS YOU HOW

The Monster.

That was all that April could see. The calmer, rational parts of her head tried to give it the name Skandis. Tried to apply functions to the various limbs and appendages. Tried to envision an environment that demanded that evolution answered back with quite so many teeth.

The problem was that the calmer rational parts of her brain were completely drowned out by the rest of her body screaming. She fell back, the thing reared over her, those terrible tentacles whipping down towards her, their jaws snapping at her.

Then time went weird.

As her head smacked into the floor, her eyes rolled up. She saw the white walls of the combat chamber. She'd already stopped noticing the walls but she could see them clearly now. They were that same, uniform, glowing white. But there was something about them. Seen from the floor, she could see how they'd been cleaned, and not very well. They were streaked with grime and little dark red trails of dried blood.

The Monster pushed down towards her. The smell was repugnant, catching in her throat. She retched, trying to roll away from the tentacles. Then she was up and running, still doubled over and gagging, her eyes streaming from the smell. The Monster swept around, tentacles hissing as they tried to locate her. She was trying to work out where the door was, but the room was just stretching away. She kept running until she bumped up against a wall and stopped, catching her breath, rubbing the water out of her eyes.

This had been a terrible mistake.

I Am Not A Soldier. I Am Not A Soldier.

She didn't want this. She didn't want to be fighting this.

She had just wanted to find out what was going on.

She had wanted to be the clever, brave one.

Now she was running for her life.

She ran.

She kept running.

I have no plan. I have no idea what I'm doing.

I will not fight it. I'm not a soldier.

Oh god. Where is my gun?

She smacked into another wall. She was cornered. She twisted round, trying to see where she'd dropped her gun. As she'd walked in, it had felt so good to be holding a gun. It was solid, it was chunky, it was heavy. It didn't feel like paintballing or Laser Quest. This was real. This could protect her. This could hurt.

Only now she'd lost it.

The Monster heaved itself towards her, slithering and lurching, rearing up to spring. Sensing victory, it paused. Tentacles flailing through the air towards her, the jaws opened. She could see those dreadful teeth, the air-meltingly awful stench of its breath.

She had an absurd urge to laugh. She was supposed to fight this thing? Who'd thought this was a good idea?

Her brain raced on again.

Up until now she'd taken this all on board. The disorientation. The endless white rooms. The complete isolation. The idea that behind this place was a great and powerful plan that really understood what was going on and was doing all it could to save the Earth.

The world was like that. She understood that. People made important decisions and other people carried them out and told more people that it had to be done and so it gradually trickled down and spread out until everyone's lives were somehow affected by it. The decisions didn't have to be good (they often weren't), they just had to be made and somehow they'd end up happening.

You could shout, you could protest, but you just couldn't stop them.

There'd been that time when it had been announced that the new wing was being built at the school. It had seemed like a really good idea. The school was getting cramped, parents were fighting – literally fighting – to get places, the classrooms were run-down, grimy, and everyone told you not to talk about the mice (Mice! How great would it be to just have to worry about mice). Building a new block seemed brilliant. Then it turned out that new blocks do not build themselves. The School had decided to sell off a little bit of land – nothing very exciting really, just a few trees and some scrubby grass in a corner of a field. It seemed fair enough. Then a parent found out that it was being sold off to build luxury flats. Luxury flats overlooking the football pitch, blocking the light. It had to be stopped. Scrapped. There was a protest. April and her mum had gone along – a few years younger and her politics had been so much simpler. She'd painted a placard that said *Save The Trees*, and she'd waved it and shouted and there'd been so many people and clearly, if so many people were cross then Something Must Be Done.

Something was done. The plans for the tower block were revised down by a couple of floors. And then, having looked at them again, the developers realised that they might just need a little more space for car parking, and so they'd need a little bit more space at the side. Just a little. And this was given to them and everyone felt pleased and then the plans were revised a third time and there was now no car park and the building had miraculously expanded to fill the space at the side. It was now bigger than ever and completely blocked the light at one end of the pitch.

There'd been another protest and obviously this time some people were more furious and others were more cautious. If shouting had worked out so badly last time, then what would happen this time? Perhaps, just maybe, they should be a little bit more wary. Just in case. But April hadn't cared. She'd waved her placard (still intact once she'd Sellotaped it a bit) and shouted 'Save the trees!' but even she'd wondered what it was all for.

'It'll be okay, won't it?' she'd asked her mother.

There'd been a pause. Her mother had squeezed her hand. Ever so slightly. 'Yeah,' she'd said. 'In the end.'

She knew now what her mother had meant. That the world changes and it changes for the worse.

On the way home, she'd carefully, neatly, folded her placard up and put it in the recycling.

Looking back on it, she was sure there'd been meetings, there'd been a plan all along. Some people had met in a room and they'd said, 'We'll do this and they'll do this and we'll play it this way and then we'll get what we want and it's for the best.' It had been talked through and argued over and debated and in the end someone made some money and the school got a new building. That was how real conspiracies went. They weren't exciting. They were a bit dull actually.

That was how things happened. She was sure that was how all this had come to pass. Someone had seen there was a problem and they'd worked out how to solve it and they'd thought it through and argued the toss and then decided that this was the best solution. Build the Void. Fight the war that way.

Only …

Well, this was the thing …

As the tentacles pressed against her skin and the teeth trailed across her skin, April screamed at the top of her voice:

'Who the hell thought it was a good idea to throw teenagers at monsters?'

ADVERTISEMENT: YOUR BOOK WILL CONTINUE IN 25 SECONDS

'Hi, I'm Todd and this is why I fight.'

(We see Todd. He's in combat gear. He's taken his helmet off, and we can see that he's ruggedly handsome, with a kindly older brother's air to him.)

'Why do I fight? It's simple.

I fight for the planet Earth.'

(Shots of green fields and sunny days and beaches, lots of beaches.)

'I fight for my parents, my family.'

(Shot of Todd's parents holding hands. Shot of his sister shooting him with a water pistol. Jokes.)

'I fight for everything that's good about our beautiful world.'

(More beaches, this time at sunset.)

175

'I fight for tomorrow.'

(Sped-up footage of the night sky, scurrying clouds, daybreak.)

'I fight because the Skandis are evil. They want to destroy us, our planet, our way of life. We can't let that happen.'

(Grainy black-and-white footage of Skandis in combat.)

'We can't let that happen. We can't let that happen to the Earth.'

(Footage of a playground. Screaming children fleeing from an unseen menace. A mother scoops up a toddler and runs towards the camera, her face full of terror.)

'We're here because we're making a difference. I don't care how long it takes. What it costs. Because I know that while I'm here, I'm doing everything I can to ensure my world is safe.'

(The Earth seen from space, beautiful, tranquil, fringed by the rising sun.)

'What I'm doing here is right. I'm Todd and this is why I fight.'

(Todd, staring straight into the camera.)

The video ended and everyone in the Big White Room rose to their feet, applauding wildly. They looked at each other, at the screen, and they cheered.

NORMAL.

THE TEN BEST ALIEN DEATHS YOU'LL SEE TODAY. #6 IS A KILLER

So what? She'd used the safe word. It was April's first time. Surely no one had expected her to do any different. Screw them.

It wasn't instant. That had been surprising. She'd had to wait the ten seconds for the dimensions to stabilise and for the chamber door to open.

Ten seconds in which she was quite sure that she could have died.

Ten seconds in which to keep fighting and keep alive.

Ten seconds in which she became aware of her heart. It was beating strangely. Beating with excitement and verve. Filling her body with an unusual amount of energy. Like adrenalin but different. More wild. The alien part of her heart. The bit linked to a Shadow Kin Warlord. The bit that said, 'I am bred for battle and I must fight'.

The pulsing heart beat so strong and fast that it spun her round, made her pick up her gun, aim it again at the nightmare. Only it wasn't so nightmarish anymore. It was just a Skandis. Just something to wipe out. That was all.

She got ready to squeeze the trigger.

Then the Skandis vanished and the combat chamber sprung open.

She heaved herself out and stood there in the bay, waiting for her heart to calm down.

'Woah,' she breathed.

April spooned down her savoury porridge flakes and wondered what the hell was going on.

How many days had she been here? Was this her first day? Her second? Her third? She felt completely disoriented and desperate to know how her mum was coping without her. She'd be worried, wouldn't she? She'd have called the police? But how was anyone going to find her – wherever here was, or wasn't.

Every morning (was it even morning?) it was the same. She'd wake up in the white room. She'd take a deep breath. She'd remember. She'd think about what she had to do that day. And she'd feel utterly alone.

* * *

'Hey everyone!'

Seraphin's face blotted out a wall of the chamber. Everyone looked up from their breakfast.

Seraphin stepped away from the camera. He was topless and holding a plate of food.

'Cinnamon toast. You want some?' He took a bite. 'Ohhhh delicious.'

Then he walked back a little bit further, sat down in a leather chair, flung his legs up along the side, tugged at his hair and continued to munch his way through the plateful, while the audience spooned slowly through their grey soup.

'Apparently the battle has been going really well. Like amazingly well. Let's just look again at some of yesterday's footage. That's right #clipshow.'

The huge wall filled with head-camera footage.

A Skandis on the ground, flailing.

A rifle butt came into frame.

It smashed down and down and down again. Each impact made a wet, crunching thud. The horrific frame of the Skandis shuddered and squealed each time, its so solid frame crumbling and shattering under the impact.

A solitary tentacle continued to twitch.

The rifle butt smacked down on the tentacle. It sheared off, flopped around wetly, then stopped moving.

The shot changed, showing flashes of arm and ragged breathing. Movement, movement, the head whipping around to show something following.

It was someone running. With a Skandis following, screaming and howling. The person running was out of breath, you could hear it catching and wheezing and desperate. It was a girl.

For a moment April thought – is that me, was that me, did I sound THAT scared?

For a few seconds all you could see was white. Then the running stopped.

Breath. Ragged breath. A shot of boots.

The girl was doubled over, catching her breath. She was exhausted. She'd given up. That was it.

The hall echoed with the slight creak of a hundred people leaning forward in their seats.

They were going to watch her die.

Then the shot changed.

She'd stood up.

She'd turned around.

She was facing the Skandis still running towards her. So close. So lethal.

She shot it.

The soldiers in the hall breathed out, cheering and clapping, fists pounding on the tables.

Wow, thought April. *Aliens vs Hogwarts.*

Wherever she looked around the room, at all the cheering faces, her helmet told her 'NORMAL'.

'Another one down!' someone shouted. No one looked around to see who'd said it. There'd been something, a little falter on the last word, that told them that they'd thought better of it.

The shot changed a third time.

At first it seemed to be a drone. A drone spinning somewhere, seeming to take off, whip up and then hover overhead, looking down at a Skandis. It swept backwards and forwards, observing and monitoring and checking in.

It flew up higher and began to slowly descend, drifting down.

It was a peaceful, gentle scene.

Then they all heard it.

The voice on the picture. The voice saying, softly and quietly, 'Please, no, please no.'

It was crying.

It drifted closer and closer. Down towards the monster. Ever so slowly.

Something moved to the left of the frame.

A tentacle. Clamped around a leg. Pulling the camera closer and closer. Drawing it in to the great, vast mouth that split open across the top of the creature.

The picture went black but the screaming didn't stop.

The wall went back to white. The Big White Room was utterly silent.

Then Seraphin spoke.

He was back there, still sprawling in his chair, not a care in the world. He put down his plate, dusting crumbs from his hands and licking the tips of his fingers. 'Delicious. Amazing. It's recipe time. Hey – you know, like when my sister taught me to make a sausage casserole. Jokes if you've not seen it. So here goes with today's recipe:

Here's a few cheeky tips for slaying a Skandis …'

April looked around at the other people eating. None of them met her eye. Flickering around the walls was headcam footage, screen after screen of food. That was it. She leaned close to the person opposite her, trying to squint with one eye, to see if the image of the boy's face appeared, however fleetingly, on the screen. The overlay in her helmet said 'ABNORMAL', urging her to look away.

Well screw that.

The boy was so young. He was pale. He had spots clustered round the straps on his helmet. He wouldn't meet her eye.

'I'll keep staring at you,' whispered April, and she meant it.

The boy carried on eating.

April carried on looking at him.

'Listen,' she said. 'Why do you fight? Why don't you try to get home?'

The boy said nothing.

His spoon hesitated, just for a moment. Then he carried on eating.

April gave in, and looked up at the screen, where Seraphin was still talking away.

'Here's what we've got,' he said, his tone as bright as ever. 'Weapons. You can't toast a Skandis without them. But it's important to know how to use them. Really lethally use them. Here are some of my sister's old dolls. Kidding, they're mine.'

He gestured to a row of plastic ballerinas.

'The gun is the easy bit. It blasts—'

A ballerina shattered.

'It burns.'

A ballerina whoomphed into a melting pillar of fire.

'And the butt – snark, I said butt – can be used as a club. That's why it's so heavy.'

The end of the rifle smacked down, breaking a ballerina into pieces.

'And, in an emergency, we've also given you an electronic stunner.' Seraphin grimaced. 'Really? Like who came up with that name and why aren't they fired?' He winked. 'We should have a competition to see who can come up with a better one, isn't that right, Captain Pugsley?' He held up a small, wrinkled, cross-looking dog. It grunted and then got back on with the depressing business of being a pug.

April slept. In her dreams she saw all the headcam footage. The endless army of Skandis fighting, lunging, attacking, the soldiers fighting back at them, advancing, screaming, dying. On both sides the slaughter went on. Overlaid over each and every frame of her dream was one word: NORMAL.

She woke up in a dark room. Only it was a dark room that she knew was white. That felt strange. Her heart pounding, she was ready for battle.

'What the hell am I doing here?' she thought.

8 WAYS IN WHICH PEOPLE HAVE TRIED TO ESCAPE THE VOID

1. The boy who shot himself in the foot. FAILED.
    The gun simply refused to fire.

2. The small group of dissenters who had tried to find a way out. FAILED
    Some said they were still walking somewhere in one of the corridors.

3. The girl who smashed up her room. FAILED.
    She came back to it after a meal to find it completely replaced.

4. The boy who faked appendicitis. FAILED.
    He woke up to find his appendix removed.

5. The brothers who refused to eat. FAILED.

   They carried on fighting, claiming their heads felt clearer without food, but insisting they wouldn't eat till they could go home. After 7 days without food, both vanished on a Level 4 combat mission.

6. The girl who said she had to go to her mother's wedding. FAILED.

   She was assured, despite evidence to the contrary, that the wedding hadn't yet taken place.

7. The guy who'd just stayed on the floor of the Big White Room, screaming. FAILED.

   He'd been taken back to his room, and hadn't been seen since.

8. The girl who got out.

   Actually, that one's a Rick Roll. Sorry.

AT FIRST SHE THOUGHT SHE KNEW EVERYTHING BUT THEN SHE FOUND THIS SECRET SHE HADN'T KNOWN SHE NEEDED TO KNOW

April wanted out. She wanted to get home. She wanted to make sure her mum was okay. More selfishly, if you'd pressed her, she would have told you that she was miserable.

After a meal break, she wandered the corridors, seeing if there was anything. She ignored the gentle way the Void had of suggesting that you went this way instead of that. Instead she strolled along, pushing occasionally at the walls. She figured that, at some point, this whole structure had to have a weak point. At the very least, someone's room would be unlocked and she could try and talk to someone. She patted her way along a corridor, turned left, went along another one, circling back towards the Combat Chambers. She didn't want to end up there by accident.

She bore left and pushed on another square of wall. Then she pressed on a little bit further and walked towards the end of the corridor. A white wall. So perfectly white. She pushed against the end of the corridor, and felt it click. Just a little. She pressed it again, and it slid open. What was beyond it was startling, simply because it was so dark. No white. Just a dim grey tunnel that blew cold air at her. She stepped into it, pulling the door closed behind her.

Was it too absurd to hope it'd end in an emergency exit sign leading to a car park? Perhaps she wasn't at the end of the universe after all, but simply in Slough. God, she would love to be in Slough. The corridor ended in a small flight of metal stairs. She climbed them.

After all the empty, futuristic concealed panels and blankness, what was most surprising about what was at the top of the stairs was its sheer ordinariness.

It was a normal wooden door.

April, nonplussed, knocked at it.

'Coming!' said a voice.

April stood there, baffled.

The door opened.

'You!' she cried.

Standing at the door was Seraphin.

WHEN SHE MET GOD SHE FORGOT
TO ASK 'WHY?'

The room was the last thing she would have expected.

It was Seraphin's bedroom.

She wandered around it in a daze.

There was his bed with its crumpled sheets. There was the shelf full of wonderfully ironic toys. There was the table with a huddle of laptops. There was the little nook leading to the bathroom with its massive selfie mirror. There was even the bay window, looking out onto …

'Yeah,' said Seraphin, 'you can poke the sky. It's fake.'

April leaned out of the window. Because he'd told her to and her head was just not up to anything else. Beneath her was just darkness. And ahead of her was a brilliant skyline which looked somehow wrong. Wrong because when you prodded it, you felt nothing. Just nothing. But it all rippled. Like paper.

'Whaaaaa?' said April and stopped talking.

'Hi,' said Seraphin, and he reached out and took her hand. He shook it firmly but not too insistently. 'You'd better not be a fan.'

'Not really. April.'

Good, 'cos if you were a fan and you'd somehow managed to get here I would, I really think, scream.' Seraphin smiled and gave a little scream.

April smiled back. Up close, Seraphin was a bit too hot to look at directly. Like a polite, sweet sun. But there was something different about him. Something that made him weirdly more handsome.

'Oh, got it! You're wearing clothes!'

'Yuh,' Seraphin ducked his head. Actually he was wearing a lot of clothes. Comfortable sweat pants, baggy slogan T-shirt, smart hoodie, and a beanie hat that suited him amazingly. 'What?' he said. 'My clothes only fall off when I'm working. You know, I just do it for the likes, the reblogs and the gifs. When I'm off duty, I like to be WARM. I like to wear a shirt. I like to be shnoogly. Especially in winter – the heating bills are PHENOMENAL.'

'Don't worry, you look great,' said April. 'I mean, sorry, I mean … god, this is weird.' She laughed and she didn't know why she was laughing. 'It's you. You're really here.'

Seraphin laughed too. 'Next thing you're going to say is I'm shorter than I look on screen.' This was clearly a joke. He was really tall and he had these blue eyes that just stared at her with keen interest and …

Wait a minute.

Wait.

'You're Seraphin,' said April.

'Yes.'

'You're here. You're not … I dunno … a hologram.'

'That's an excuse to fondle my chest, right?'

'No. No! It's just … Are you in charge of this place?'

April stared at him sick with horror and the realisation that she'd basically just walked into the villain's lair. If a villain's lair had more ukuleles than normal. Wow. She'd been so stupid.

Seraphin threw back his head and laughed.

'Sorry,' April practically gushed with relief. 'Sorry. I just assumed that you were in charge.'

'No. But can you imagine? Me?' He tore off his beanie hat and threw it onto the desk and shook out his hair. 'Look, who are you?'

'I came because of your messages. We decoded them.' At the 'we' Seraphin looked reassured. 'And I came here to find you.'

'Oh thank you, you're amazing!' Seraphin whooped. 'I've been stuck here for months.'

'Stuck here?'

'Help, I'm A Prisoner In A War Game Factory!'

'So who is behind this?'

'I don't know.'

'Really? So you don't work for them?'

'Oh, I work for them, but that's NOT THE SAME THING. Not at all. Listen,' he threw himself onto a Swiss ball and started bouncing it around the room. 'Dead truth, okay. I was offered a contract, to be the public face of the site. It was, well, it was a tonne of money. And it was for charity. So, you know, I said yes. They explained about the mock-up of my flat and everything and that was totally cool. I get that some people like artificial. But then I get here, and I think it's an afternoon filming a few inserts and so on ... And I Have Been Here For Months. And it has got weirder and totally weirder and do you want a juice?'

He reached under the desk and threw her a small box of fruit juice. 'Even here I still get freebies. Insane.'

'What flavour is it?' April said automatically, and then smiled at herself.

'No idea,' said Seraphin dryly. 'I do know that it's vegan friendly and gluten-free and that if you enjoy it the PR firm encourage you to tweet about it using the hashtag #sosopure.' He smirked ironically.

'Right.'

April stabbed the straw into the carton and wondered about what she was going to say next.

'Where is here?' she asked.

Seraphin threw his hands out, wobbled on the ball, and righted himself. 'No idea. Like there was an Uber. I got in it. Well, I thought it was, only ... Anyway,' he bounced forward on the ball, grinning wolfishly at April (a very polite, house-trained wolf). 'You say your people decoded my messages?'

'Yes.' Oh, this is where it was going. Oh dear.

'And you've come to get me out.'

'Ah.'

Seraphin took the news reasonably well. Sort of. Eventually. Once he'd stopped shouting. April might not have entirely helped. She was doing her best at looking both contrite and calm when it suddenly struck her that she was a soldier trapped in an alien dimension inside a fake flat with a celebrity shouting at her on a space hopper.

'You're laughing!' Seraphin broke off his rant, incredulous. 'You're laughing?'

'Well, yes,' April said. 'Sorry.' She blew her nose and then tidied her hair back. 'You have no idea – how scared I am, how much I want to go home. I need to get back to look after my mum. I need to tell my friends what's going on here. Oh god, there's so much I need to do. And I thought that you'd ...' She laughed again. 'I thought that you'd have a way out.'

'And I thought that you did.' Seraphin laughed too. 'The whole situation is crazy. We're all stuck here. I'm still doing all my normal vlogs from in here about "My Insane Life" and it's all about the sunglasses I'm being paid to wear, a healthy snack delivery company I've been endorsed to discover, or a song I'm writing or whatever, rather than what's really going on, which is so mad. Like, if ever filming your daily life should be about something, it should be about this – massive space war against fricking aliens. Shouldn't it?'

'Well, yes.'

'The saddest vlogs are the ones that are about something. Vlogs by sick kids.' Seraphin wasn't laughing. He just looked so sad. 'Jeez. I can't stop watching them. They're not even popular – just grim. Kind of like *Game Of Thrones* grim, you know? But I am an addict. 'Cos people are all like, "Hey Seraphin, you're so brave putting yourself out there," and I'm like "Thanks" but I'm not a kid stuck full of needles.

But yeah, dying. That's not Living The Dream.' He grabbed himself another juice and tossed one across to April.

'The whole vlogging thing's really hard, you know. My Insane Life. Everyone looks at you like they know you. And it's like, "You may think you know me but I do not know you" but when they run up to you at a music festival you have to be all smiles even when they jab you in the face with the selfie stick. 'Cos you've already made the choice to be their best friend. That's part of the mission. If I'm out in public, then I'm always on. I'm always smiling.

'And you learn, like, when you really commit to it, that the sun always has to shine. 'Cos it's my job to tell you that it's okay. That life's great. Is your life?'

April blinked. 'Well, no, I mean, sometimes not, but you know …'

'Nah-har.' Seraphin made a Wrong Answer noise. 'That's your audience gone. Not what we came here for. And, don't get me wrong, so many of my problems are #FirstWorldProblems.' He stopped, shifted posture on the Swiss ball, and suddenly bounded into a devastating impersonation of himself. 'Hey guys! My hair! Dis-as-ter! Like whaaaaat? Insane! What am I going to do with this? Oh shoot me!'

He slid off the ball and landed on the floor. April had never seen someone do an impression of themselves, and it was odd. Ten seconds of sharp self-hatred.

'I'll tell you the things I don't get to do. Simple things. When you commit to doing this every day, you don't realise that there are going to be Bad Days. Or you think that you'll store up a few so that you can have a few days off. You know. But that never happens. It just doesn't. And then, you know, top secret, but when you have a hangover, you don't get to crawl back under the duvet. You have to share it with the world. Share! It! With! The! World! And your hangover has to be funny and here I am in Speedy's Café and I am so in need of bacon and isn't that great and …' He gave a long, thoughtful sigh. 'I'll be wearing a baggy jumper that makes me look vulnerable yet adorable. Think about that – I have to pick what I'm wearing when I'm hungover.

'And, hey – you ever been dumped?'

'Ack,' said April.

'Sorry,' said Seraphin. 'I know, right, I've only just met you. Too much sharing. But it's like, you're dumped. You wake up the morning after and you just want to not be awake. Like getting out of bed is impossible. Iron Man is sat on your shoulders. But no. You gotta get out of bed. And the worst thing is that you wake up and you are dumped and then you remember that Everyone Knows. Literally everyone. Like, if it happens in public, in a restaurant, someone will have live tweeted it, and there'll be three reaction videos out there already. And you don't get to have a day off. You have to be out there and be dumped and be nice about it.'

'I think,' said April, 'that's called being a gentleman.'

'Yeah, very good, 1950s.' Seraphin's laugh was a non-starter. 'But is it fair? Sometimes, I just want to get stuff off my chest. 'Cos they were doing my head in and whatever, but I have to be sooo still. Even – you remember the one who released an album about me?'

'Not really, no,' April admitted. As much as she was aware of Seraphin, she sort of had a vague 'dating that model with the quirky handbags' memory. 'But you're famous. Worse, you're internet famous. Some woman goes out with you, she's going to be hated. She breaks up with you, she's going to get so much more hated.'

'Yeah yeah yeah,' Seraphin agreed wearily. 'Jeez. Sometimes I think the whole online thing was invented just so we could hate on women. But look, hear me out, right. Say I'm single, and I go out and I meet a girl right, the morning after she'll post "So, this just happened ... " with a picture of me asleep in her bed. And the world just goes BANG. Like what? I've not got control over that. Like, I can't say I've got a cold without three different PRs biking me over their client's cough meds and a little note suggesting a hashtag. You know, I just want it to be back to when it was just fun insane rather than insane insane.'

'Like this?' suggested April.

'Totally.' Seraphin scrambled up, and kicked the wall of his flat. It wobbled. 'This is the point that it's all gone totally nuts.'

'What the hell do we do now?' asked April.

THIS IS YOUR CHANCE TO WIPE
OUT SKANDIS FOR EVER

'COMBAT CHAMBER EMPTY.
BATTLE READY TO COMMENCE
SMILING EYE'

After leaving Seraphin she'd tried fighting again. And again, she'd not got any further.

What the hell was this place? Was it even a place? Was she trapped in an idea?

She'd thought that finding Seraphin would have helped. Like Dorothy finding the Wizard of Oz. Only the man hiding behind the curtain wasn't pulling any levers. He was simply there to make a lot of noise.

He'd tried to help her, but hadn't really been able to do much. It was like neither of them had a full picture of what was going on. He was there to get brave people to fight monsters in order to save the planet. She was there, supposedly, to fight monsters to save the planet.

But something didn't link up between the two.

So she'd gone to fight a monster, to see how it made her feel.

'That's definitely a reason why I don't want to do this,' she grunted as a Skandis threw her against a wall. Was she imagining it, or was the wall less padded than yesterday? Was the Skandis more aggressive? Was she finding it a little harder?

She lay on the floor, panting and tasting blood in her mouth. 'I'm not a coward,' she said, and activated the safe word.

The next ten seconds proved she wasn't a coward. The ten seconds it took the dimensions to normalise and for the Skandis to vanish were endless. As if sensing the fight was over, the Skandis threw itself at her with desperate energy. April fired off a shot from her gun, more as a warning than anything else. It singed the creature's hide, making the slime bubble and steam as it scorched its way through the flesh. The creature roared, pulling itself up.

'I can do this,' April thought. 'I can do this after all.'

She raised the gun. Aimed.

And the creature vanished.

* * *

She staggered out of the Combat Chamber. She was soaked in sweat and shaken. She held a hand out in front of her and watched it tremble. She took a deep gulp of breath and tried to hold it, but she couldn't.

Another soldier was standing there, visor down.

'Are you okay?' he asked.

'Yes …' she said. 'Just … shaken …'

'Sure,' he said, sounding concerned. But not taking the helmet off. He just carried on staring at her. I'm being filmed, April thought. I'm looking at him and my screen says NORMAL. He's looking at me and his screen says ABNORMAL. I'm being filmed through all of this. I'm going mad and I'm fighting aliens and I'm being filmed. If I crack now, if I go crazy with this guy, then he'll just be filming all of it. And it'll be shown in a loop. A loop of 'This Weak Girl …'

She stared back at the guy.

'Hey,' she said, and she held up her hand. 'Look, it's shaking less. Woop-de-doop-dee.'

'Yes,' said the soldier, after a pause. How old was he? Mid-twenties? Ten years younger? The helmet made it impossible to tell.

'Just, you know, still getting the hang of it.'

That creature, rushing at her out of the whiteness, roaring and spitting and leaping. And her gun coming up and her dodging to the left and then the right and the thing still coming at her.

'Yeah,' the soldier said. He wiped a hand across his sleeve. There was that strange green blood/fluid all over it. 'Just killed one. They take a while. You're Level One, now, yeah?'

'Yes.'

'Wait till you get to Level Three. That's when it gets pretty juicy. They're really fast moving there. And they take longer to kill. They're really vicious.'

'Vicious?'

'Vicious.' The helmet made the guy's face implacable. 'The Level Ones are much slower. Like they're older. Or not so good at fighting.'

'Okay.' That sounded odd.

'Sometimes it's like the Level Ones are actually pleased to be killed. Imagine that, eh?'

'Yeah.' April was finding this whole exchange odd. 'So ...' she said.

The visor tilted at an angle. Curious.

April very carefully said nothing.

'Do you want to go back in there?' the soldier said. 'I know how to re-jump the Combat Chambers ...' He gestured to an instrument panel at the end of the bay.

'We're not supposed to know how, but they're really easy. I can pop you back in there in a couple of minutes.'

For a moment, his soldierly air had been replaced by boyish enthusiasm. He was almost dancing over the instruments. A boy showing off to a girl.

'No, you're good,' said April. On the one hand, maybe it would do her good to confront her fears. On the other, there was something about this that just didn't feel right.

'You sure?' The visor looked at her, once again unreadable.

'Yeah, thanks,' said April. She walked away.

She knew now what she had to do and that it wouldn't be easy.

April walked into the Big White Room, joining everyone at the meal that was possibly breakfast.

She chewed on the soapy flakes, plucking up the courage. The moment passed. Another moment passed. And then, in a rush, she pushed her bowl away and stood up.

'I want ...'

She faltered. She swallowed, raised her voice, and stared again. Everywhere she looked was wrong.

'Everyone, I want to talk to you about the Skandis. I'm not going to fight them anymore.'

She'd wanted a reaction. No one said anything. Spoons lifted food from bowls.

The video of Seraphin played on.

'I'm not a coward,' she shouted to the room full of people who were ignoring her. That's not an easy thing to do. 'I'm not saying I don't think the Skandis are evil.'

No one cared, but still she carried on talking. 'I'm just saying that I don't get why we are being made to fight them. It shouldn't be us.'

The volume of the video went up slightly.

'*Cupcakes, eh? I love cupcakes. Today I'm going to make some amazing cupcakes and cut my own hair.*'

'Like that!' April raised her voice till it scratched at her throat. 'We should be doing stupid things. Like that. Normal things. Not ...' She stopped, lost for words.

'*These scissors ... Do you think they're blunt or Psycho badass? As in Stab! Stab! Stab! Arg!? And do you think I'll get hair in my cupcakes? Well, Captain Pugsley will decide.*'

A square appeared, blocking out a tiny, stamp-sized portion of Seraphin. It was a small picture of April. Someone in the room was looking at her. Just one person. Someone was paying attention to her.

April kept talking. 'This. This room. Think about it. Please. This roomful of people. Isn't it insane? Isn't it wrong?'

'And now we're gonna clean the bowl the best way. Giffers go crazy at me licking my batter.'

Another square appeared on the huge screen. Two people. How many before ABNORMAL became NORMAL?

'Look around you. Look up. Stop looking at him. Look at yourselves, at what you're doing.' April hoped her voice didn't sound desperate. She was going for strident, she was going for confident, but those last words, something pulled at her vocal chords and choked them slightly.

'Still plenty of cream in the bowl, so a big dollop for Captain Pugsley and oh, oh, oh, I've spilled some on my chest. Classic.'

More squares appeared. More small pictures of April, breeding and multiplying, spreading across the wall. People were looking at her.

'Listen to me,' she shouted at them. 'Stop fighting. Stop this madness!' Then she filled her lungs. One final push. 'JUST LOOK AT ME!'

As she said it, she realised she'd made a terrible mistake. Gone too far.

For a moment it was all good. The picture of Seraphin broke up entirely and the screen became one big April staring back at her. Waiting to hear what she'd say next.

And then, one by one, as her words echoed around the room, those squares blinked out. The wall was whole again.

'Three second rule, dammit, Captain Pugsley!'

Too needy. She knew she'd lost them. She turned around and walked out.

AFTER YOU READ THIS YOU'LL WANT A SHOWER

April woke up. The room was wrong somehow. For a moment she hoped she was back in her bedroom at home. That it had all been a dream. But that wasn't how dreams worked.

The room was dark. Completely. It went this way when you were supposed to be asleep. It was disorienting. She'd woken up in the dark here before and it was peaceful. This time though, there was something wrong in the room. Something that itched. Something that refused to be right.

She heard the breath.

She was not alone. There was someone in the room.

She realised how wrong she was when they came for her. About a dozen of them. Rushing towards her. She cried out and then they were on her.

The attack wasn't long. It could, she told herself long afterwards, have been worse. They didn't even hit her with weapons. Or fists. Some of them grabbed her sheet and pulled it tight. She couldn't move. She struggled there, helpless, refusing to scream. They struck her with the flat of their hands, blow after blow on her face, her body. She looked up as long as she could, her eyes not seeing their faces, just the helmet cams staring at her.

I'll never know who you are, she thought. I'll never know who did this.

She ignored every urge to shout back at them, to beg, to cry with pain. She felt her heart, that strange part of her leaping around in fury. Something deep inside her wanted to hunt down everyone in this room and kill them all. She hoped it was the alien part, and not her.

The blows stopped. She sensed people stepping back. She felt a moment of relief.

Then she was reeling from a terrible rank smell. It was so overwhelming she fought back for the first time, struggling against the hands holding her down.

What have they done, she thought, they've let a Skandis into the room. They're going to kill me with it. I've said I wouldn't fight and now they're going to make me fight.

Something landed on her. Wet. Repulsive. As it touched her skin, she felt it flare up and burn slightly.

Her eyes streamed and she gagged at the terrible, sticky, dirty smell.

The hands holding her down released her. They stepped away. They walked out.

The door opened. The door closed.

The lights flickered on. She knew they would. She knew what she would see.

The dripping, severed face of a Skandis was pressed against her mouth.

Looking back, from a long distance away, she realised that neither she, nor her attackers, had said a word.

It had been a long night. The lights in her room hadn't gone off. Repulsed, she'd eventually squirmed her way out from under the head. The bedsheets were stained with a mixture of slime and blood, seeping over the sheets and into the mattress. Inside the tiny room, the smell was choking. Of course the door was locked.

The head sat on the bed, watching her with boiled-egg eyes, the tentacles flopping and slipping over onto the floor. She moved to another corner of the room and curled up in it and tried to close her eyes. It didn't work.

She remembered the pillow and slowly, reluctantly worked herself up to go back for it. She hoped that the Skandis's blood hadn't touched it. That would have been something. But no, of course, the pillow was covered in tiny, foul smelling spots of gore, burning into the cheap foam inside.

So April just sat in a corner and tried to ignore the severed head and stayed utterly, chillingly calm. The smell became more and more overpowering and she could hardly breathe without retching, but she stuffed a fist into her mouth and screwed her eyes shut. She didn't think about the pain she was in, she didn't think about what had been done to her, she didn't think about what she'd do next. She just waited and waited. Until eventually the door sprung open.

She'd hoped the shower would have done something about the smell. The stench of that decaying creature was in her hair. She swallowed mouthfuls of the tepid water, trying to clear the taste from the back of her throat. She checked herself for bruises – there were none. They'd been careful. Nothing to make anyone feel any sympathy for her. She stayed in the shower until the water slid from tepid to lukewarm to cold and then she got out. She caught sight of herself in the mirror, and her mouth fell open. She made a noise. A half-sob from somewhere deep inside that, if she'd let it continue, felt like it would never stop. She stifled it.

She dried herself on the cheap towel and slipped into a fresh uniform.

Walking towards the Big White Room was the hardest thing she'd ever had to do. At least, she told herself, there'll be no surprises. I know they're all waiting there. They know I've been humiliated, hurt. They'll all know.

But it's a meal. It's a day.

She breathed in. Be brave, she told herself. You can face them. You can face them all and that's how you win. Don't even put your helmet on. Don't hide behind it. Just look at them.

She walked in.

There was no one in the room. Nothing on the screens. Just empty benches.

No food.

She wandered around for a bit. Forced jollity. She swung her shoulders around. Then the exhaustion, and something else pricking at the edges of her eyes, wore into her and she picked a bench and sat down.

Someone walked in. They were wearing their helmet, their face tilted down. Was this one of her attackers? The boy walked over and sat down a few seats away from her. His nose twitched.

God, thought April, I must still reek of that thing. She fought down the urge to apologise to him. Almost automatic, but not.

Another boy walked in.

Then a girl.

Then another girl.

All of them silent, heads down, not noticing her. This was nothing unusual.

Her strange heart fluttered and she wondered if this was them – the group of people who'd assaulted her. *Kill them all, just in case.* The alien thought passed through her head and was quickly discarded.

A boy walked in. Taller and broader than the rest. He sat down opposite her.

They all sat there. Nothing happened. No food turned up. Nothing.

They were all around her. But no one was looking at her. They kept on doing it.

Unable to bear it anymore, April sprang to her feet. She wanted to run off, to shout, to say something, but she couldn't think of anything to say. She stood there, glancing from bowed head to bowed head.

It's like I don't exist, she thought, and then sat down. She knew then that she was trembling. She pushed her hand out in front of her and watched it shake.

This is really, really getting to me, she thought.

More people filed in and sat down. None of them looked at her. I'm nothing to them, she told herself. And

212

that's okay. I can work with that. So long as I can get rid of that thing from my room I can go back there and I can wait this out. No fighting. Seeing no more of these people. Just living is enough.

But what if they come back to my room? Maybe I'll leave the head where it is, after all. That should keep them out. But when can I go? When can I leave?

More and more people filed in and sat down and kept on coming until the room was full.

Still no food.

Just waiting.

Come on guys, thought April, the war's not going to fight itself. And look at all these people – no porridge. How they going to lift their guns?

The giant screen flickered into action.

'Morning everyone!' Seraphin was hanging upside down from a pull-up bar, waving. 'It's someone's birthday today, so we're going to celebrate their special day. Let's hear it for April, the birthday girl!'

Everyone in the room burst into applause. A strange, terrible, clapping in unison. April flinched from it.

The clapping stopped.

'Apparently you got her a surprise cake! Am I right? I'm right. Hope you saved me a slice!'

The screen cut to the severed head landing on her bed.

And then back to Seraphin. 'We're lucky to have you April. Let's give her another hand!'

And he stayed there, frozen on the screen.

Little squares replaced him. Tiny shots from headcams as one by one everyone looked up to stare at her. All of them. Every one. A thousand Aprils filling the room.

She stood up, stumbling as she tried to push back the bench. But there were too many other people, holding it down with their own weight. She backed away. And watched the action repeated from every angle.

Seraphin's voice called out, 'Who's got a magic memory of April they want to share?'

And then, from every angle, she saw the assault on her from last night. Repeated over and over again. As Seraphin sang 'Happy Birthday'. Her face, twisting from side to side. The blows falling on it.

'It's not ...' began April, stammering. She tried again but the singing continued. 'It's not my birthday!' she screamed. Suddenly this point seemed really important to her.

All that happened was the giant wall carried on showing her face crying.

'It's not my birthday,' she repeated softly. 'And I'm not going to fight. You're not going to make me fight.'

This turned out to be a lie.

YOU'LL BE AMAZED AT HOW LONG IT TOOK HIM TO REALISE HIS MISTAKE

'It's about April,' said Ram. 'She's missing.'

WAR VETERANS ARE COVERING THEIR HEADS IN GLITTER FOR REASONS THAT WILL STUN YOU

'COMBAT CHAMBER EMPTY.
BATTLE READY TO COMMENCE
SMILING EYE'

'I'm not giving in,' April told herself. 'I'm just showing them. Showing them what, I don't quite know.'

She picked up a gun, steadied it, and took a deep breath.

The readout counted down. The dimensions stabilised.

Then, with a tiny click, the door slid open.

April stepped through into the Combat Chamber. For a few moments it held its warm, vanilla-scented emptiness, and then the landscape flickered into being across it.

Everywhere she looked, projected onto the floor were rolling marshlands and sulphurous pools. On the walls were distant hillocks and thundering clouds. Above her more clouds drifted across the roof. The temperature fell and the air took on the tang of bins on a hot summer's day.

April shivered and walked on. Looking around, she realised this was the first time she'd seen the alien battlefront. The strange no-man's land that they fought in. She tried to taste the air – an artificial representation of an alien atmosphere. This may have been only a simulation, but it was a simulation of an alien planet. Every step she took here was somehow echoed on that planet. She was both here and standing somewhere far beyond in space. This was thrilling.

Yes, but not thrilling enough for her to forget her sense of defeat. Just by being here she'd given in. She'd admitted that she was going to fight. Was this how the machine rewarded her? With a better simulation of her alien surroundings? A little treat. You gave in, have some virtual reality.

April walked on, feeling the floor sink slightly under her – was this an illusion, or was it … she reached down and patted it – soft rubber? Clever. Squinting she could see it followed, just slightly, the contours of the land projected onto it. She moved on a little further. Judging from the feeling on the back of her calves, she was walking down a slight slope. She glanced back – the doorway had receded and she seemed to be at the bottom of a hill.

Impressive. But also worrying. What level was she now at? The terrain wasn't flat. There were rocks, weird, burnt rocks – anything could be hiding behind them. She moved forward, and the marshland receded to a silvery shore, which edged its way up to an ochre cliff. This was it, she guessed. She turned back.

Somewhere around here, something was going to come and kill her.

April trudged on through the mire. Increasingly, she'd stopped thinking of it as some kind of illusion, and let her head tell her that she was on an alien planet. Flashes of wonder filled her mind. *I'm on an alien world.* What made her convinced that it was real was that she was finding the whole thing increasingly tiring. Her legs ached, her bruises hurt, and there was sweat pricking and trickling its way down her back. Is this what it was like for astronauts, she wondered? Amazement at being where no one had gone before, followed by an annoying slight itch in their space boot?

She skirted the edge of the swamp, her boots crunching along the silver pebbled shore. Her feet hurt, but this was also really pretty something. The thick, wrong-coloured clouds carried on drifting slowly over her (were they going the wrong way? Was there a wrong way for clouds?). She stumbled slightly against the rocks and, with nothing better to do, sank gently down onto her back.

Here she was, looking up at space clouds in an alien sky. Glimpsed beyond them were whole new stars, shrugged into totally different formations.

Her life had changed a lot over the last few weeks, but this really was it. Alien Planet.

It had been a bit of a rush. Of course aliens existed. She knew that, but had always thought of them as a vague possibility, in the same way that she knew that Russia existed. Then aliens started turning up at her school, armies of them, and the sum total of everything she knew got very hard to keep a hold on.

April had tried making her own rules for life. They weren't glamorous, or complicated, or even that ambitious. It was her way of saying to the world: 'You took my dad away, you crippled my mum, and you broke everything I believed in, so, from here on in World, it's going to be baby steps'. Her rules had been based around looking after her mother, trying to ensure they didn't talk about it too much, making sure they weren't talked about, and trying to impose some small little bits of normality on life. Which aliens had, literally, driven a bus through.

Her carefully settled world had been shaken up like a snowglobe. New rules, new heart, and now here she was, some kind of teenage super-soldier, fighting aliens. It was all ridiculous. Exciting, but ridiculous. She thought she should probably stop before it got out of hand.

She laughed at that. And then, lying on her back on a not-quite real alien marsh beach, she started to hum a song to herself.

A few minutes later, she dozed.

The buzzing woke her. Her helmet was making little *fzz fzz fzz* incoming text message vibrations.

She blinked and was startled by the clouds wandering over her.

'ABNORMAL'

Right. Yes. Alien Planet. Beach. Dozing.

Fzz fzz fzz.

Why was her helmet doing that?

Maybe whoever monitored the helmet camera. If the shot didn't change, that was a bad thing. Either she was dead or not putting on enough of a show. Maybe that was it.

Fzz fzz fzz.

She picked herself up, now feeling every bruise, and shook her head. Her helmet was still buzzing. She looked up the shore and then realised why her helmet had been trying to get her attention.

There were three of them.

Three Skandis, slithering across the beach towards her.

April crouched, grabbed her gun, and started backing away.

She'd come to fight them, but now she was here, she was wondering. She'd just wanted to take on and kill one, to make a point. To show the people outside that she was as good as them.

But where would that get her? If she survived, she'd shown that she would kill. Wouldn't they just make her fight again? Wasn't she being manipulated?

Of course, she'd thought she could probably kill one of them.

But three?

Three of them coming towards her very quickly.

There was no way she could kill three of them.

Coming here had been a terrible mistake.

The three creatures swept along the beach, the stones skittering and popping as their tentacles and claws scraped over them. Whereas they'd initially moved in a group they were separating – one continued to glide towards her, another rolled into the marsh, and the third sprang up to the edge of the cliff where it climbed across the rocks at a terrifying rate.

April realised what was happening – they were herding her. If she backed away she was losing the advantage.

Losing the advantage? What am I like?

No. She needed to hold the line. *Hold the line?*

The three Skandis were really close, tentacles whirling up into the air.

'This isn't my fault,' she said to them. 'I don't want to do this.'

She raised her gun.

'I mean it,' she shouted, the cliff swallowing her voice. 'I will kill you.'

She felt her heart, her weird heart, pounding in her chest.

The creatures pushed closer.

Something moved up on the clifftop – more of them. Come to watch the slaughter.

She could smell them, that terrible reek of death and vinegar.

April stood there, holding the gun. She raised it and aimed it.

'I will use this,' she said. Was she talking to herself or the creatures? She sighted one of them, and marked its drop points. *Drop points?*

A tentacle whipped past, stinging her cheek, burning her. She cried out.

'I will use this,' she said.

She squeezed the trigger, firm constant pressure.

Nothing happened.

She squeezed the trigger again.

Nothing.

What had she done wrong?

April held the gun out to the creature, almost as if asking it where she'd gone wrong.

The Skandis brushed it out of her hands and launched itself down onto her.

THIS ICELANDIC PENGUIN VILLAGE IS PROBABLY THE CUTEST PLACE ON EARTH. BUT YOU ARE NOT THERE

The three Skandis exploded in ribbons of burning flesh. One moment they were there, the next they were three meaty fireworks, shooting limbs, offal and sparkles of gore across the beach.

A dense cloud of foul smoke engulfed April. It stung her eyes and poured into her mouth. She gagged and choked, staggering back, rubbing her sleeve into her eyes.

What had just happened? What the hell had just happened?

With a wet patter, the last burning remnants of the creatures pattered onto the beach.

April lurched away, blinking to clear her eyes.

Then stopped.

Amazed.

'You?'

Miss Quill was standing there with a gun.

'I cannot tell you how good that feels,' she announced, blowing across the muzzle of the gun. She stopped, frowning slightly, considering her options, and finally allowed herself a small, brief smile.

'Killing things feels good. No, it feels *really* good.' Miss Quill rocked back on her feet, surveying the red-green mist of body parts.

April loved her keyboard. Without it she couldn't work through her thoughts and turn them into music. But sometimes, when she was thinking too fast, she'd hit too many notes and the keyboard would just stop trying to keep up and emit a single thin sharp note. It was her keyboard's way of saying 'Enough, April. Stop!'

Right now her brain was making the same noise.

She'd just seen three creatures killed.

She was covered in stinking flesh.

Her gun wasn't working.

The Skandis had been killed by Miss Quill.

Who was somehow here.

What was going on?

Wait, back up a minute. There was something wrong.

Miss Quill.

Had killed them.

With. A. Gun.

April blinked.

Miss Quill was aiming her gun at her and the smile had turned into a grin. 'Funny thing,' she purred. 'I saw the creatures attacking you and I wondered. I mean, they'd given me a gun but I had no idea if it would work. What with the creature in my brain that's supposed to stop me from using weapons. But there you were. About to be killed. And, oddly enough, because of the interdimensional fields, it turns out I can use weapons here. Isn't that peachy?'

When April replied her voice was ridiculously calm. The Queen At A Garden Party polite. 'And are you going to shoot me?' she asked.

'Oh, I'd love to,' said Miss Quill. 'But, sadly, I've come a long way to rescue you. I doubt I'd get any thanks if I brought you back dead.' She tilted the gun up and looked at it wistfully. 'No more fun for you, you poor little thing,' she actually cooed at it. 'It's a very nice gun,' she remarked. 'Lovely aim, simple action, strong result, stunning battery life. Not that you'd appreciate these things,' she smirked. 'You'd be too busy being all "Oh no, a GUN, euw, euw, euw, I must start a petition against it and maybe paint a little sign about it".'

'That's not fair,' protested April. 'I tried ... I tried to shoot one of them. Just now.'

'How long have you been here?' Miss Quill asked.

'Days,' said April.

'And you've only just managed to not shoot one of them?' Her eyebrows arched. 'How you lot ended up as Apex Predators I don't know. I guess evolution has a wicked sense of humour.'

For the first time in a long while, April felt a familiar emotional reaction. Trying to talk to Miss Quill both made her want to smile and stamp her foot. (Did anyone, ever, actually ever stamp their foot? Still, that's how she felt.)

'Look,' April said, 'it's been difficult.'

'I'm sure it has,' Miss Quill oozed. 'No scented bath salts or organic delicatessens here. You poor thing.'

'How did you get here?' April asked her. A change of subject sometimes helped.

'Does it matter?' Miss Quill acknowledged the move and fended it away effortlessly. 'Let's get you out of here and tucked up in your no doubt achingly princess bed. You can drink camomile tea and compose a really scathing review for this place on Airbnb. Come on,' said Miss Quill and marched off.

'Right.' April breathed out slowly and set off after her.

She couldn't believe it. She was leaving behind the shore, the alien corpses, this whole nightmare. She was going home.

'Oh.' Miss Quill stopped and spun round. 'You know what? I just can't resist.'

She shot April in the head.

IN THE TIME IT TAKES YOU TO READ THIS SKANDIS WILL HAVE CLAIMED 100 MORE LIVES

April woke up.

Again?

She was in a small white room. Charlie was there.

Charlie smiled in her direction, using his warm, distant, seriously polite smile. 'April,' he said with the formal courtesy of someone still trying to get used to forenames. 'You are all right.'

'Miss Quill—'

'Is outside. Keeping watch.' Charlie sat down on the edge of the bed. He squeezed her hand, a very gentle, reassuring pressure.

'She shot me!' April protested in a whisper. Knowing Miss Quill, she could hear through doors.

'I know,' Charlie whispered back. He did not seem to be taking her entirely seriously. 'She was disabling the camera in your helmet. We've removed it. You're now off the network.'

'Oh,' said April. 'She could have warned me.'

A small 'Hah!' came through the door.

'It is not her way.' Charlie's smile became rueful. Then he looked more serious. 'Why did you come here? You have put yourself in great danger.'

At first April thought how sweet that was. Then she remembered that she was an unwilling pawn in an intergalactic war. If she died, so would her timeshare heart, and then who knew what would happen to the Shadow Kin? Was Charlie's concern actually for her at all, or simply for the balance of the cosmos?

'I had to do something,' she protested, and hoped that didn't sound at all pathetic. 'You were all talking and debating and people kept going missing. I couldn't ignore it any longer.'

Charlie frowned and turned away from her. He was looking at the wall, which was odd as there was nothing on the wall.

'I see.'

'Do you?' she persisted. 'It's just that something needed doing.'

Charlie nodded.

'You acted as a leader,' he said.

'Oh.' April blinked. 'Well, I suppose so. Something was wrong and needed sorting out and so I ...'

'Led,' Charlie finished.

'Not exactly.' April wondered why she was so defensive, and why Charlie seemed so hurt. 'I mean, I'd hardly call it great leading. I've not done much except get shot at.'

'Leaders do not always make great decisions,' Charlie turned to her, smiling sadly. 'But they make decisions and others follow them.'

'But ...' Others? What others?

The door opened and in came Miss Quill, Tanya, and, obviously, Ram.

Tanya did the explanations.

Miss Quill announced that the room was crowded.

Ram looked at April for some reason. And, for some reason, April looked back at Ram.

Tanya explained that it took a couple of hours before they noticed she was missing. 'And we realised why you'd been acting so strangely, and that the whole system could be gamed and that obviously we could do the same ...'

* * *

VIDEO CLIP UPLOADED TO TRUTHORDARE.
COM
(also available as a rather popular animated gif with
the caption: 'THIS IS HOW MUCH OF A TOSS I
GIVE')

Tanya, Charlie and Ram in a rollercoaster. Tanya and Ram are
screaming their heads off in giddy terror. Charlie is screaming
in pure horror and alarm.

At the front of the carriage is Miss Quill. She is completely
calm, bored even, apart from a very slight smile. She is reading
Captain Corelli's Mandolin.

'Anyway, once we'd done that we came right after you.'

'Long afternoon,' said Ram. Was there candyfloss on
his shirt?

'Afternoon?' April said.

'And quite a late evening,' Ram said. He was
sounding defensive, in the unique way that boys have
of sounding defensive when they know that somehow
they've done something wrong but aren't sure what.

'Wait!' April sat up in bed and winced. 'I've been here
DAYS.'

'No,' Tanya corrected, 'hours.'

'But—'

'Hours,' Miss Quill confirmed. 'This is a slow dimension. It has all sorts of benefits.' Again, that troubling smile. 'All sorts. They've been able to assemble a fighting force capable of taking on an entire species using, really, little more than a handful of humans. Let's face it, they'd need all the help they could get.'

April took a moment to process that. As in, to stop her brain thumping against her eyes. Her friends had not forgotten about her, they'd not abandoned her, she'd been worried about her mum for no reason. It was all going to be okay. Apart from that they were trapped in another dimension. Yeah, that bit still sucked.

'So, what do we do now?' April asked. 'I mean, you've come here to rescue me. What's the plan? How do we get out of here?'

There was a moment of blank silence.

Then Ram coughed awkwardly.

'The thing is … um … Now that we know what the Skandis are, we were thinking of fighting them.'

'I don't believe it,' cried April. 'Seriously?'

'Well.' Charlie was looking at her very firmly. 'The thing is, you've kind of taken the lead on all this, so well, we're open to suggestions.'

'Well, one option,' said Miss Quill, 'is to win the war. Have you thought of that?'

'No,' said April. 'I'm not sure that war is the answer.'

Miss Quill uttered a long, loud groan. 'I really do think you're the worst,' she drawled. 'Perhaps we should all sit around making placards. We could stroll onto the battlefield waving them. I'm sure both sides would listen. Maybe you could make up a lovely little song as well. Something we could all sing while they're launching everything they've got at us.'

Disappointingly, Tanya and Ram were nodding. 'We saw some training footage,' said Ram, 'before we could come looking for you. Those creatures – they don't look pleasant.'

'Pretty grim,' agreed Tanya. 'Demon zombie octopus.'

'Much as I'd normally call this parochial speciesism, I have to agree,' said Miss Quill. 'The Skandis have to be wiped out. They're heading towards the Earth. What do you think they're going to do when they reach it? Hold a car boot sale?'

'That's not the point,' April argued. 'I think this is all about perception. What have we been told about them?'

'That they're going to destroy the Earth,' said Ram.

'Do we know that that's what they're doing?' April said. 'I mean, has anyone in this room – the non-humans – heard of them?'

Charlie and Quill glanced at each other.

'Well, no,' admitted Charlie.

'Isn't there an intergalactic Wikipedia?' April pressed on. 'Something you can look them up in?'

'Let's go check Wikipedia!' Miss Quill tutted. 'What a typical student response.'

'But, if they're a race of predators, wouldn't you know about them?'

'The universe is best assumed to be a hostile place,' Miss Quill said firmly. 'If strange craft appear in your system, man the defences and start shooting.'

'Isn't that a bit short-sighted? How does it go down?'

'Not at all well. But if your visitors are intelligent they will see it as a perfectly sensible response. You humans flatter yourselves that you have the monopoly on brutality and greed. You don't.'

'Well, I think we need to find out more,' said April. 'Think before we shoot.'

'Oh, look at Miss Moral High Ground,' laughed Quill. 'What were you doing before I rescued you?'

April looked at the floor, suddenly angry. 'I was in a combat chamber. I was trying ... I was trying—'

'You tried to shoot one of these monsters. I saw you,' Quill said triumphantly.

April looked up and knew she'd lost the room.

'Yes!' Tanya was grinning. 'This is what all these evenings of World of Warcraft have been leading up to,' she said. 'Finally I get a proper gun.'

'No,' April insisted. 'Tanya. Can't you see that you shouldn't be doing this?'

'I shouldn't?' Tanya's face set hard quickly. 'Because I'm younger than you?'

'No! None of us should be fighting. Why isn't this scheme picking on adults? We can't even vote but someone thinks we're the best to fight an alien war. That's …'

Tanya groaned. 'Look, it's an outsider's view – maybe not the right one, but someone's decided that we're the best people to fight this thing. So maybe we should.'

Ram nodded, and April felt her stomach sink.

'If there's one thing I've learned, these last few weeks,' he stumbled, 'it's that the rest of the universe is pretty mean. And it seems to have no problems killing kids.'

'Exactly, Mr Singh,' said Miss Quill.

Tanya nudged Ram in the ribs. 'Come on. I'm going to get a gun and find out how this system works. You game?'

She pushed on the door and went out.

Well, thought April, about a minute ago I was in charge. That didn't last long.

Ram stood there, hesitant, hanging back but obviously eager to go. 'Just so you know,' he said, sounding a bit mumbly, 'Tanya has a point. If those things are coming for the Earth then she's right. I don't want to say I stood by and let it happen.'

'Sure,' April said, not even looking at him. She didn't even have to try to make her voice bitter. 'Absolutely. Go fight your war.'

'Yes,' said Ram, going for a joke. 'Tanya'll so think we're best friends now.'

He went through the door. April looked up. 'Is that how you think women relate to you?' she wondered. 'Side with them, they'll get a crush on you?'

She turned back to Charlie and Quill.

'Well,' she said to the two of them. 'I think I can guess what Miss Quill's going to do.' She pointed to the door.

Miss Quill barked with laughter. 'Are you sure?' she said. 'Really?'

'Yes,' April said firmly. 'You're going to go and slaughter those monsters.'

'I'd considered it,' Miss Quill admitted, 'but I've come up with something a little bit more fun.'

And then she raised her gun and pointed it at Charlie.

239

MANY PEOPLE WOULD BLAME THIS ON MARRIAGE EQUALITY. BUT WOULD YOU?

They came in from the day's kills exhausted. They were sweaty, grimy and bleeding. Their helmets hung limp from their hands, broadcasting swaying, unusable footage of the floor. The troopers poured into the Big White Room, all of them thoroughly, utterly shattered.

Some had been here for weeks. Some only for hours. But the fighting was getting worse. Whereas previously the battle computer had normally sent them into combat with only one, or maybe two Skandis, they were now up against groups of anything from three to a dozen.

To start with, it had been a bit more fun. A change was good, after all. They called it 'levelling up' and those who came back boasted of having Done The Boss. The problem was that fewer and fewer of them were coming back. And troops who'd levelled up found themselves going straight back into combat.

If they'd been expecting a different scenario, or to encounter Skandis with different weapons or something more novel, they were disappointed. There were simply more of them. And they were angrier and more vicious.

When they'd thought war was a bit like a game, then it had seemed thrilling. Now every hour of every day was spent going through a door to fight more and more of the enemy. It would only stop for rest breaks, for food and for sleep, and then it would start again.

The ones who lived were the ones who thrived on the routine. They took even more risks, they found the familiarity comforting, they pushed back against it, but they never forgot the skills they'd learned.

The ones who didn't come back were the ones who found it boring. Who found it draining. Who thought that it was unfair. You weren't banned from complaining about the challenges over your helmet camera – that was fine, although it might be edited out of Seraphin's recaps. What was curious was that, if you did complain, your chances of stepping through the door into a battle with five or six Skandis rapidly increased.

The Learning Hour was becoming grimmer. The troops sat around, trying to keep their eyes open, as vid after vid slid past them on the great wall. Sometimes they saw themselves and cheered. Sometimes they saw friends and realised they'd never be coming back and they booed the enemy. They hated the creatures they were fighting against, and they did it with an instinctive, weary, ingrained hatred. The more routine, the more dull the war became, the more they'd carry on with it because they had to. They were, though, Seraphin thought, becoming a tougher crowd. It was harder to get a laugh out of them.

As the broadcast switched on he looked out across the hall at all their faces – teenage faces scarred with combat, with dirt burnt into them and massive purple bags under their eyes. They looked gaunt and wired. Somehow it was his job to keep them going. And he just wasn't sure that he wanted to anymore.

'Heeeeeeey! Evening everybody!'

Seraphin was standing in his room. He had piled his hair up on his head, and was laughing. 'I'm henna-ing my hair. What is up with my life? I'm almost out of cereal. Anyway, how's the battle going? We've some really good kills going on here today. Some excellent kills. Really lovely stuff. Shall we have a montage? Yeah, let's … wait—'

Seraphin stopped and licked his lips. For a moment, just a moment, he seemed uncertain. Curious. Brave.

'Hey, have any of you lot seen April recently? You know, the trouble-making one? She's fallen off my radar. Hope she's okay. If any of you see her, you'll let me know okay? Right. Anyway. The latest fighting. Cue clip show.'

Scenes from the day's battles played across the huge screens, accompanied, for no reason other than he enjoyed it, by Seraphin playing 'Climb Every Mountain' on his ukulele.

Charlie shouldn't have been surprised. Not really. Ever since he'd been assigned Quill as his bodyguard, he'd known that she would someday point a gun at him. In theory her head should right now be exploding with pain. It wasn't. She was simply holding the gun without even the slightest wince. Actually, she was smiling a proper, warm smile. Any second now she was going to kill him.

At moments like this, Charlie felt like the loneliest person in the universe. He'd lost his family, his friends, his world, and the only person left who remembered them was his bitterest enemy – his reluctant bodyguard, who wanted, more than anything, to kill him.

Charlie was not unaware of the irony. It was made more curious by the mode of speech that humans used. They were persistently violent in conversation, which often confused or alarmed him. When someone would say, 'My mum is going to kill me,' he couldn't help automatically picturing Miss Quill pointing a gun at him. That image haunted him. For once, when a human said something, he knew exactly how they felt. A curious sensation of dread, of inescapable inevitability. Sometimes he forgot about Quill's nature, sometimes they were almost like friends, with more in common with each other than anyone else on the planet. But that image was always there to remind him. Because one day, she'd find a way around her processing and shoot him.

In some ways it was a relief. Having Quill point a gun at him felt like being able to breathe out at last. There it was. As suspected. Yet, at the same time, he felt a twinge of disappointment, regret. As though, maybe, in their time together they'd become … well, not fond of each other, no, but still that they'd developed some sort of bond.

All the same, it wasn't stopping her from aiming that gun.

'Yes, I know,' Quill was pouting sarcastically, 'how dare I? Quite easily. Now, are you going to beg before I shoot you? I think it would be nice.'

Charlie said nothing.

Quill raised the gun, finger tightening on the firing trigger.

'Come on, Prince,' she coaxed, purring. 'Just a few little last words for your slave.'

245

Charlie was silent a moment longer. 'Actually,' he ventured, 'I have got something to say.' And he said two words more.

April burst out laughing. Posh people swearing, there and then, became her favourite thing ever. Quill glared at her.

'Sorry.' She cupped a hand over her mouth. 'Sorry, Miss Quill, you can go ahead and shoot him now.'

'Thank you.'

'Surprised you've not done it already.'

'When I need your advice, girl, I'll ask for it.'

'Totally. And I wouldn't dream of offering it.'

'Oh really?' Quill paused. 'You look just the type that loves giving out unwanted advice. Some children think they're so grown-up and really, they're not. You know nothing about life.'

'No,' admitted April. 'I don't. But I do know you won't kill Charlie.' Charlie glanced at her, curious.

'What?' Quill hissed.

'You would have done it already.'

Quill stared at her.

'You've been waiting to kill him for months and yet, there he is still breathing.'

'So?' Quill was curious.

'Go on. Just shoot him,' April urged. 'Sorry, Charlie.'

'No, that's fair.' Charlie's voice was even calmer than usual. His posture shifted, with regal delicacy, and he leaned forward, into Quill. 'Go on. Do it.'

She stared back at him.

April began to have doubts about how this was going to end. She'd assumed that she was right, that Quill was bluffing – she wouldn't really, she couldn't really, could she? She talked all the time about it, but she wasn't really a cold-blooded killer, was she? April remembered the three Skandis exploding on the beach. Or maybe she was wrong.

'One word,' said Quill, eventually, that little smile back on her face. 'I just want to hear one word from him about how sorry he is – about what he did to me, about what happened to my people. And then I'll let him go.'

'You'll pull the trigger,' Charlie corrected. He still seemed icily calm.

'Well, yes,' Quill admitted. 'But you'll die knowing you're the better man. That's what you love, isn't it?' she sneered. 'The moral high ground. Slavery and slaughter that you can feel smug about.'

'You keep saying that you are my slave.' Charlie's calm carried on until even April felt infuriatied. 'You are not my slave. People buy slaves because they want them. I appreciate you, what you do for me. But,' and the calm got a degree chillier, 'I do not want you.'

'Suppose there was another way?' began Quill. She seemed to have stopped blinking. April wondered if she actually needed to blink, or if it was just something she did to appear more human that she'd forgotten about. Come to think of it, Charlie wasn't blinking either. The two were just staring at each other like chess players. With a gun.

Charlie picked up Quill's sentence. 'If there was another way to keep me safe? Then yes, I would happily take it. And we would both be free of each other.' He smiled a very calm smile. 'I'm afraid that is all you are going to get out of me.'

The two stood there. Quill pointing the gun. Charlie, head tilted back insolently, eyes daring her to do it.

'See?' Quill turned back to April with a helpless shrug. 'Even at gunpoint, even in the last moments of his life, he cannot say sorry. He is just impossible. And the more human he becomes, the worse he gets. Unbelievable.' she rolled her eyes, dropped the gun and walked out.

April let out a breath she didn't know she'd been holding.

Charlie picked up the gun and looked at it.

'Are you okay?' April said to him. 'After all that? Are you sure you're okay?'

Charlie turned to her, baffled for a moment, and then smiled the dazed smile he used for trying to understand a joke.

'Ah,' he said, and pointed the gun at his head. It clicked. Nothing happened.

He passed it back to April.

'It's genome-locked,' he said. 'It's set to only kill one species – the Skandis.'

'You knew?' She was incredulous.

Charlie was nonplussed. 'It was a reasonable surmise. Humans are, forgive me, violent. Genome-locking the guns is a safety precaution to prevent the soldiers here turning on each other or on whoever runs this facility.'

'But you were absolutely certain?' April continued, amazed. 'You knew that she'd not be able to use the gun, that she'd not found a way round that. Did she know that you knew too?'

Charlie continued to examine the gun placidly. 'Oh, she may have guessed. She may even have disabled the lock, but, there's one thing you have to remember.' He looked up at April and his eyes were sad and serious. 'Ever since she was assigned to me, I knew that sooner or later she would point a gun at me. From day one, I have been rehearsing what to say.'

PEOPLE ARE TWEETING THEIR WORST BATTLES AND IT IS CRINGINGLY HILARIOUS

April's hopes of escaping were fading fast. Instead, her friends (and Miss Quill) had fallen in line with the place.

'Is it just me?' she thought. 'Am I the only one who doesn't want to fight these things? Am I being incredibly dense?'

She wondered if she was just being stubborn. But then she figured, what did it matter? Surely they'd get tired of it in an afternoon or so, and, as long as she kept a low profile, she'd not get into any trouble. Once they realised how serious the battle really was, they'd come up with some way to get out of here.

Ram hurled himself across the battlefield.

Three Skandis? Fine. Bit of a challenge, but nothing he couldn't handle. He was loving shooting at them. Okay, he made sure that he downplayed how much fun it was to April, but the whole soldiering thing kept on giving him a kick. Especially when they played footage from his head cam on the Big Screen. He couldn't help it. He felt proud.

'Is it wrong to feel so pumped?' he asked Tanya over the evening meal.

'Pumped?' She shook her head. 'Next thing you'll be saying this food is nutritionally amazing.'

'Well,' he had to admit, 'my stomach is looking pret-ty flat.' He spooned down some more of the weird porridge gloop. 'Probably a mixture of no sugar and all the running.'

The running was the best bit. For some reason, out here, wherever they were, his leg had shut up. It just did what he asked, and tried not to get in the way. It was like having his old leg back, only it glowed in the dark slightly.

'The running.' Tanya gave a sudden smile. 'It is pretty awesome. This is like the best game ever.'

'Totally,' Ram agreed. 'Actually being in the Combat Chambers, it's amazing. And the way that the forcefield set-up prevents some of the damage. That's great.'

'What?' Tanya asked.

'On Level Four. You get a forcefield. Oh,' his face fell comically, 'are you not on Level Four yet?'

'Tomorrow,' Tanya mumbled the lie. 'I'm levelling up tomorrow.' She watched Ram chewing his slurry and tried not to resent his success. 'Wow. Level Four already, that's great.' It sounded hollow as soon as she said it, but Ram didn't seem to care. He just nodded and started scraping his spoon around his bowl.

The envy she felt was blocking her head from focusing. Why did you only get a forcefield on Level Four? Surely that would make more sense for the new recruits, progressing through the training assignments?

Then Tanya realised. Whoever was running the experiment had some limit on their resources. They only protected the more advanced soldiers because they were actually protecting their investment.

'Wow, that's cynical,' she gasped.

Ram put down his bowl.

'What?' he said.

She told him. He looked nonplussed. 'It sort of makes sense,' he argued. 'In a way. Like it's only worth getting a proper football kit if you're playing for the team.'

Tanya stared at him. 'This place is changing you,' she said.

Again, he looked slightly baffled. 'It's an experience. Experiences change us. It's how you grow up.' Gawd, he could sound so dull. He lowered his voice, speaking out of the side of his mouth as he chewed. 'You shouldn't be talking to me here, Tanya.'

'We're still not friends?'

'Yeah, there's that, sure.' Ram looked at her seriously. 'But also, remember – people don't really talk here. It would look … strange. For us to be seen chatting together. They might check the camera feeds.'

'And deduct points?' Tanya was starting to feel cross. The kind of cross that even though a bit of her head was saying 'Woah, hold on, he's maybe got a point' the rest was steaming.

'No, no.' Ram hadn't even noticed. 'I mean, a bit, yeah, but they might crack onto us. Currently you're showing up as NORMAL. I'd hate for that to become ABNORMAL.'

'Woah.'

'Anyway,' Ram shrugged. 'Are you going to finish that food?'

'You're welcome to it,' said Tanya, stood up, and walked away.

Ram slid her bowl over, and started to eat happily.

There was one combatant who had entered the system recently and already reached Level Six.

She did not fit the typical profile of the Skandis Recruitment Programme.

She did not fit it at all.

Yet she was here. A little older. A little taciturn. Maybe she didn't come to the Big White Room to watch the inspirational videos. But she had come through the system and she was turning out to be the best recruit they had.

When they'd initially processed her, they'd considered her a statistical oddity. So much so that they'd come to her room at night, stepping through the walls to question her in her sleep.

'Name?' they'd asked her.

'Quill,' she'd said.

'Firstname or Surname?'

'Just Quill,' she'd insisted.

She was certainly a blip. But a blip could be useful, if she lasted a few rounds. As it was, she'd lasted rather more than a few rounds. Her progress was faster than anyone else in the challenge, and she was accounting for more kills than many of their other contestants put together.

They came for her at night again.

'Why are you so good at this?'

'I like killing.'

'But what are your allegiances?'

Quill snorted, or it may have been a laugh.

'You fight as though you really believe in the cause.'

'No,' Quill mumbled absently through the dream shield. 'As I said, I really like killing.' She smiled in her sleep. 'Oh, how I've missed it.'

That gave them pause for thought. They'd somehow, accidentally inducted someone entirely outside the programme's remit, someone they'd normally have discounted entirely. And yet, she was proving to be their best asset. Perhaps they'd need to revise their recruitment parameters.

'We were never here,' they told her. Then they went away.

'That's got you puzzled,' muttered Miss Quill as they left.

Ram saw Charlie coming out of a Combat Chamber and rushed up to him, punching him on the shoulder.

'Look at you, Princeton! You've settled into fighting after all.'

'Yes,' said Charlie, without any hesitation.

Ram chuckled. 'Knew it, knew it,' he laughed. 'Once you start playing, you can't stop. What Level are you on? Have they given you a forcefield?'

'No,' Charlie considered. 'Why, have you got one?'

Ram leaned forward. "Course I have,' he laughed. 'Anyway, catch you later!' He aimed a couple of practice shots at Charlie and then bounded off down the corridor.

Charlie watched him go without blinking.

April laughed. 'He really thinks you're fighting?'

'Well, at least someone does,' Charlie said.

'And, just checking, you're okay that you're not?'

'Yes,' said Charlie. 'Sure. Absolutely.'

He settled down at the edge of her bed. 'Definitely.'

They'd had to reach a compromise. One of the problems was that Quill didn't want Charlie going off into combat without her, just in case her brain exploded. Charlie did not fancy going into combat with Quill, just in case she managed to carefully, accidentally, catch him in a ricochet. April didn't want anyone going into combat, but especially not Charlie. ('If I'm right,' she argued, 'you could start some kind of interstellar war.') So Charlie had quietly agreed to fluff his Level One assignments. He'd fluffed them so spectacularly that footage from them had made it into a vlog called 'Soldiers Do The Funniest Things'.

Then he'd gone to see a soldier who he'd assumed was in charge of the Combat Bay. 'Look,' he'd said, 'it turns out I'm useless in battle. Really. It's so frustrating. Is there anything else I can do?'

When Quill found out she'd laughed herself sick for a minute.

'You're a cleaner?' she'd roared.

'It is a practical and necessary function,' Charlie reasoned. 'There is no disgrace in it.'

'Oh, of course not, your majesty,' Quill had hooted.

When he'd scrubbed out her chamber that night, he found the walls elaborately painted with entrails. He spent several hours scrubbing off an elaborate and ancient Rhodian curse.

SHE DROPPED A TRUTH BOMB BUT WASN'T EXPECTING WHAT WOULD HAPPEN NEXT

They were eating their evening meal when April walked into the Big White Room.

'Hey!' she called, and her voice shook. 'Me again.'

On screen, Seraphin carried on talking. He was wearing an old rabbit onesie, strumming away on a guitar and listing troop manoeuvres.

She walked into the centre of the White Room.

'I know you can't see me, but I ask you to hear me.'

The scraping of spoons around bowls became louder, the heads more bowed.

'I've come to open up, to bear my soul, to confess.' She shouted the last words, feeling her throat rasp. She had to carry over all those spoons.

She glanced at the screen. One square was her. It dipped and wobbled. Tanya. Another square sprang up. Charlie.

'We cannot fight these aliens. Not until we have more information.'

A third square. Miss Quill. She was sat just over from her and was looking disapproving. If a facial expression could convey 'I am only doing this because I was told to' then hers did so most clearly.

'I repeat. I cannot kill these creatures. It's insane. We're being sent out to fight a war and we're just not up to it. We're kids.'

The moment she said it, she knew she'd got the wrong word. She'd wondered about 'children', she'd spent about a second on 'teenagers'. Quill had suggested 'cattle'. That would have been better than hearing 'kids' echo back off that great big wall.

With only three squares on it.

Ram.

Where was Ram?

She spoke again, and there was a quiver to it. 'I'm not killing these creatures, and neither should you.'

'Really?'

Above her, Seraphin put down his guitar, pulled up his droopy bunny, and leaned into the screen. He stared down at her and his expression was strange. There was no smile, no glint in his eye. He was pissed off. Worse. April's father had read a book about parenting. Ironic. The thing he'd learned from it was to say, 'April, I'm not angry with you. I'm disappointed'. Apparently it was a 'coping response' for when situations got heated. Another coping response was to drive your family into a tree. April hadn't been disappointed with him about that. She'd been very angry.

Seraphin looked disappointed. His face was a master class in disappointment. It was a glorious manga doodle.

His expression stopped April in her tracks.

'I thought you were different.' His voice was very quiet, flat. 'I thought you were someone to watch.' He exhaled, a little puff of air that pushed against a strand of his perfect hair. 'You came here to tell us you wouldn't kill these monsters?' He was sneering. 'That's not what your helmet cam says.'

The screen filled. Shaky footage of April running and stumbling along the shore, the three Skandis throwing themselves howling towards her. Her recorded breathing echoed around the White Room, along with her whimpering. Surely she'd not made that much noise? Surely she'd not been that loud? Surely she'd been calmer.

The Skandis lunged at her, tentacles snapping open to devour her.

Screen April brought up her gun.

The three creatures exploded.

Screen April lowered her gun.

'Looks like you were happy enough to kill three of them,' said Seraphin. And his lips were twisted with bitterness.

'No!' shouted April. 'It wasn't like that. I've been edited!'

'Puhlease,' Seraphin sighed, 'you're not on Big Brother.'

April turned back to the room, desperate. 'I didn't shoot them. I didn't. You have to believe me.'

A spoon scraped in an empty bowl.

Another spoon.

Then more. An echo of spoons and bowls.

April carried on shouting, over the clattering. She was desperate, angry, seeking out the faces of Tanya and Charlie. But not Ram. Where was he?

She caught Miss Quill's eye, who mouthed 'boo hoo' at her. Because of course, she would do that.

April stopped shouting. But the scraping of spoons and bowls continued.

Seraphin's voice carried over it. 'Do you know why she had to kill them? Do you know why you all kill them? Because they are evil.'

The screen showed clips. The last moments of fighters, struggling and screaming against the Skandis. Those snapping jaws, those sharp tentacles dripping blood.

The spoons paused. The hall fell silent.

Everyone was staring at the screen. Rapt.

'Enough of the coward,' Seraphin's voice spoke again. 'Let's see what's been happening with our Level Six fighter. That'll bring the mood up.'

The screen showed Skandis after Skandis, a whole squad of them, being blown into screaming embers. Someone in the game was clearly very good.

April caught the expression on Quill's face. Pride.

'That is someone we can be proud of,' Seraphin's voice echoed over jets of fire melting tentacles. 'Someone who is doing all they can to save the planet. To save us all from Skandis. And if you're not on board, well ...' He leaned out of the screen to address April, from the walls, the ceiling, the floor. 'Why don't you go away?'

April stood her ground for longer than she thought she'd manage. One breath. Two breaths. On the third, she turned and ran.

THIS YOUNG FOOTBALLER HAS SOMETHING SURPRISING TO SAY ABOUT RACIAL PROFILING

'Hey,' said Ram.

April hadn't bothered to close the door. There hadn't seemed any point.

She was slumped against the sharp frame of her bed, staring at the empty white wall, and swigging from a bottle of water.

She hadn't been expecting Ram. She wasn't sure who she'd been expecting, but not him. God, what was he here for? Was he going to give her a lecture? Tell her how she was letting the side down? Is this the talk he used to give when a player wasn't up to it on the team? Gentle, sad, coaxing, grown-up? Oh spare me, she couldn't bear it.

Ram leaned against the wall and slid slowly down it. He looked so strange in the combat gear. Weirdly adult.

'Hot right?' Ram laughed, then stopped to sniff his armpits. 'Also, I really stink. Like maybe my sweat is masking the smell of slime.'

April smiled back at him. It was the weakest smile she'd ever managed.

'Been fighting?'

'Oh yeah,' Ram grinned. 'It's the biggest high ever. It's so real.' He wiped some sweat off his forehead. 'What we've got back home ... nothing on this. Football's great – but really, it's ...' He dramatically lowered his voice, 'just pretend. There are no stakes in it. But this, this is real, and I can be good at it. Not like Charlie's weird space thing. This is something we can be a part of, rather than just get dumped on.'

Ram's eyes were so clear she couldn't help but believe him. He was so sincere. He wasn't even trying to undercut it, or make light of it. He was so firm about it that she saw his reading of the world. Aliens had taken everything he understood about life away from him. They'd both lost so much to them. No wonder he was enjoying fighting them so much. It was his way of evening the score. No, she realised. It was Ram's way of winning.

'You didn't look at me,' she said. She didn't even realise she'd said it until the words were out there. She hadn't wanted to ruin the moment. But no. She had. How very April.

'What?' Ram was certainly looking at her now, confused. Guilty?

'I went to the White Room to give my speech. You didn't look at me. The others did. Even Quill. But not you.'

'Ohhh.' Ram frowned, then smiled sheepishly. 'Right. That. Sorry. I forgot.'

'Sure.' April then realised what he'd said. 'You *forgot?*'

'Well,' Ram's face squirmed, 'I knew it was on. Sort of. Just, I was offered an extra fight session, and I figured you'd be okay without me. How did it go?'

'How did it go?' April repeated. 'Look at me. I'm sat against my bed trying very hard not to cry. Have a guess.'

'Oh. Right,' said Ram. He slid across the floor to sit alongside her. 'My dad has told me that in situations like this it is best not to say anything. So I won't.'

'Fine,' April nodded.

They sat in silence for a bit.

'Only …' began Ram.

April looked at him.

'Only,' he began again, 'it was a surprise incursion and—'

'Stop it!' shouted April. 'I can't believe you.'

'Okay,' said Ram.

This time the silence held.

'I am so cross with you,' April said. 'Ever since I've been here, I've felt so alone.'

'We came looking for you,' protested Ram.

April silenced him. 'Yes, you came looking for me. And that meant the world to me, but already you've changed. You and Tanya are having the time of your lives battling aliens. Quill's become the Terminator. And that's not what this is about. I thought you'd understand. I've got my friends here and I feel more alone than ever.'

Ram rested a hand on her shoulder. It landed with the caution of a man who is worried it will be pushed away. April did not push it away.

'You were right. You really do stink,' she said.

He grimaced. 'Yeah, I'd best go run a shower.' He made as if to get up, but clearly wasn't going to.

'Don't go,' said April, pointlessly. 'You finally turn up, you may as well do some good.'

'Cool,' said Ram because he couldn't think of anything else to say.

April edged a little further along his arm.

'You think when all this is over, they'll let me keep the uniform?' Ram asked.

April smirked.

'What?'

'I'm not sure how that'll go down on the streets of London.'

'Ohhhhh.' Ram's face fell, and he shook a fist. 'Damn you, racial profiling. It's quite something when a kid can't go to school in combats waving a gun around.'

They smiled at each other.

'Not even as fancy dress?' he asked.

'Not even as fancy dress,' she confirmed.

'I was going to say I'd better make sure I've got some really great photos of this, but I'm not sure how that'd look if the police ever searched my computer.' His face fell. 'Or my mother. Which is more likely.' He changed the subject. 'Anyway, the talk – I'm gathering it went badly.'

'Stitch up.' April raised her bottle of water in salute. 'Total stitch up.'

'Sorry,' said Ram. 'If it cheers you up, I found out what Charlie, the great Royal Alien Prince is doing.'

'What?'

'They've got him cleaning,' Ram snorted. 'He's been pretending all along that he's fighting. But I caught him coming out of a Combat Chamber with a mop and bucket.'

'Woah.' April tried to picture that. 'What did you do?'

'Kicked over his bucket,' said Ram.

'You're the worst.'

They smiled at each other until April broke away, her expression haunted again.

'What?' Ram asked. He'd been about 15 per cent sure he was about to get a kiss, which was odd.

'Total stitch up,' April repeated. 'They had a video prepared. They'd edited it to make it look like I shot those creatures. And they sent you off fighting so that you wouldn't be there, counting that it would upset me.'

'And,' she stood up, 'they were right.'

She heaved the thin mattress off the bed, threw the pillow at Ram, and then tried lifting up the bed frame.

'What you doing, She-Hulk?'

'Tear that pillow apart,' ordered April, giving up on the bed and turning to the wall. 'I'm trying to find a bug. They're not just watching us in the helmet cameras, they're watching our rooms.' She tried putting a fingernail in between two wall panels. Nothing happened.

Ram did not tear the pillow apart. Instead he put it back on the bed along with the mattress. Then he found the sheet, uncrumpled it, and fitted it onto the bed surprisingly neatly.

'What are you doing?' said April. 'I need you to help me open this wall.'

'No, you don't.' He laid a hand on her shoulder. 'You need to take a deep breath and let the crazy out.'

'But …'

'Deep breath,' he said, holding up a finger.

April took a deep breath.

'Now,' Ram spoke gently, in measured tones. 'We've been transported to a different dimension, where time is running slowly, and we can be projected into an alien war. Given they've got that technology, do you think they're going to put bugs in the light bulbs?'

'There aren't any light bulbs,' April said.

'Exactly.' Ram decided to overlook that she'd breathed out. 'They've built the technology into the walls. Or it's in the air. Whatever. It doesn't matter. They need to keep an eye on us at all times – to find out who they can trust. That really freaked me out at first.'

'At first?' April blinked. 'What about now?'

'I realised they only care if you're a good fighter. And I'm a very good fighter. They know I'm loyal and I love the fighting so I don't have a problem with it. I want to hang it with you? Who cares? So long as,' he squirmed again, but it was a really intense squirm, 'so long as you don't have a problem hanging out with me.'

'No,' April said. 'I don't.'

'Fine,' said Ram. 'Then I'm going to go and have a shower, then go back and slaughter some more Squid. And Little Miss Dissident?'

'I'm going to find out who's really running this place,' she said.

YOU ARE BEING LIED TO ABOUT DOGS

When April entered Seraphin's room, he was playing with his puppy. He was wearing a battered old fisherman's jumper and ripped jeans.

'You look really good in clothes,' said April.

'You've got a nerve,' said Seraphin, coldly. He stood up, and switched the dog off. It vanished.

'Oh.' April blinked in surprise.

For a moment, Seraphin said nothing. When he looked up, his face was twisted, angry. 'I believed you. I fell for all your crap.' He shook his head, disgusted.

'It wasn't crap,' April insisted.

'I saw the video,' he said, getting angrier with every word. 'Everyone's seen it. There's no hiding the kind of person you are now. You're a killer, just like everyone else.'

'It's a fake!' protested April.

'Really?' Seraphin laughed. 'What? Did someone quote you out of context? Is that it?'

'No, of course not,' she said. 'That really isn't it.'

She crossed to his desk, pushing her way through the piles of musical instruments and cereal bowls. She waved the mouse, waking it up, and looked intently at it. 'Where is that video?'

'Well, it's not my screensaver,' Seraphin muttered. He poked through some folders and summoned it up.

April let it play out, following herself across the beach. Then she hit pause.

'This is the moment,' she said. 'This is the moment that I panicked, and tried to fire my gun. So yes, I tried to defend myself. But I couldn't. Because my gun wasn't working.'

Seraphin stared at her.

'Someone wanted my last thought to be that I'd given in. Now,' she nudged the video along. 'In the next frame, here, we have three Skandis all burning.'

'Uh-huh,' said Seraphin.

'The point is that you don't even see me fire one shot, let alone three.'

Seraphin frowned. 'But if you didn't fire, who did?'

April relaxed. He was thinking about it. He'd stopped completely denying it. 'You might find this surprising, but the shots were fired by my teacher.'

'Your teacher?'

'The Level Six Combatant. Or, as we call her, Miss.'

'Her?' Seraphin whistled. 'I wondered how she'd got in here. Wow. Bet she takes missing lessons really seriously.'

'Yeah,' said April, relaxing a little bit more. 'She takes everything pretty seriously.'

'Sheesh.' Seraphin called up some footage. It showed a row of Skandis being mown down. 'I'm kind of glad she doesn't teach me.'

'It is not that much fun,' conceded April.

Seraphin stood up, tugging at his hair. He was chewing on a strand of it, and twirling some of it round and round his fingers. 'So this video of you was a fake?'

'Yes.' April was firm. 'I sort of hoped you'd not done it,' she smiled. 'I'm glad.'

'God no,' Seraphin said. 'I've enough on my hands editing my own videos. For this stuff I just take what I'm given. It's worrying, isn't it? The whole mantra of putting it all out there ... It's being dicked around with.'

He crossed to a fridge and rifled through it. 'Smoothie?' he asked her. He tossed her a small plastic bottle of strawberry and banana. She opened it and downed it in three mouthfuls.

'You have no idea,' she took a last gulp, 'how good that tastes.'

'Oh I do,' he said, wiping his mouth. 'Mine had kale in it.' He tossed the bottle, with perfect aim, into a recycling bin. 'Take another. They send me crates.'

'Who sends you these?' she asked, opening another one. God, something with flavour. Amazing.

Seraphin shrugged. 'Could be the owners. Could be the people who make the smoothies. Product placement really sells. You want to take some back for your friends?'

April thought about it. 'I doubt they'd take them. Probably think I'd poisoned them.'

'Won't they interfere with your calorie-controlled fighting diet?'

'What?' she laughed. 'The stuff they feed us? It's rank. It's porridge and stew and sometimes a bit of both.'

'Oh,' he said. 'I was told you're all on a specially targeted diet. I've got some crisps somewhere.'

'Amazing.' April sat down on a chair laughing. 'I've missed chewing. It makes us all weird, having to sit and down our slops while you work your way through all this proper food. Kind of angry.' She stopped, caught up in a thought.

'What is it?' Seraphin asked her. His brows were doing that strange, kissable thing that they did. He was now doing a textbook baffled pose.

'I'm wondering about the food,' said April. 'I think they've been putting something in it. I've been skipping it as much as possible, but the others ... I wonder if that helps explain why they're so into the fighting.'

'Yeah,' Seraphin didn't sound convinced. For his money, everyone going out there seemed to be fairly pumped up. They didn't really need any more stimulants. But, if it made it easier for April to make her peace with how her friends were behaving, then fair enough.

April caught the nagging doubt in his eyes, and nearly asked him about it. Then she caught herself up before she went too far. She did not want to seem paranoid and crazy.

'The thing is,' she said eventually, 'we need to find out a bit more about the people who run this place. So tell me everything you know.'

THE LATEST ADVANCES IN VIRTUAL
REALITY WILL HORRIFY YOU

Ram was running through the Combat Chamber, loving the more advanced feel of the environment. Now he was at Level Five, everything felt so very real – you could barely even notice the walls anymore, the surroundings had lost that milky quality and every object was hyper-real. There was even the feeling of branches whipping by you – which was something totally new. Ram realised it had been days since he'd seen a tree. There really were no plants in the Training Void. Nothing other than the white boxes, the white overalls, the white helmets. It was like the only colour, the only life he saw was running through here. God, it felt so invigorating.

He almost couldn't remember a time when he hadn't been hunting here. His old life – the life that he really should have been wanting to get back to – seemed less real than the planet around him. He blasted down another of the Skandis, and laughed as it fell back, flailing and screaming. They really were the worst things in the universe. He didn't feel bad about killing them – not even a small qualm, no matter what he told April – it was like feeling bad about killing rats or wasps. They didn't add anything to the world. They were just disgusting and brutal and the thought of them reaching the Earth made him sick with fear. The Shadow Kin had been bad enough, and they'd just torn through the school. He tried to imagine the streets filling with Skandis. The image was absurd for a moment, then completely terrifying, as they'd just start killing and keep killing.

How would they arrive? he wondered. They didn't look like they'd have spaceships. They didn't show any signs of any technology. They just attacked viciously. He couldn't really imagine things like this sitting down to invent the wheel.

He blasted his way through another two, and then a third Skandis roared up, lashing out at him in outrage. Which was fine, as his forceshield would protect him. Only it didn't. The tentacle knocked him into the air and then came crashing down onto the ground with an impact that winded him. The Skandis launched itself at him, and he only avoided it by twisting to one side. His ribs ached and his lungs refused to draw breath. He crouched, his head full of fight-or-flight and unable to reach any higher thoughts.

The Skandis bounded after him, sending Ram scrabbling up a bank of skittering stones. His boots refused to find a purchase and he was spinning in mid-air. He threw himself further up the bank, grasping at rocks, pulling himself out of reach. The Skandis sprung towards him, and Ram let go, slipping down the rocks.

And then he fell through them.

That was odd. He flailed as he sank through the stones and then they vanished and he was falling through air until he landed on the floor. The air was knocked out of him again. Stunned, he lay there for a moment.

The one Skandis was stood still, its wet skin pulsing. It wasn't preparing the spring. It seemed to be scenting the air, taking in its surroundings.

For a moment, the air fizzed, and the creature looked like Neil. Neil with his scalded face, burnt red and bubbling.

Then the air fizzed again, and the Skandis was back.

Ram felt a jolt, as though a plummeting lift had just snapped to a halt.

What the hell?

He forced himself to his feet, only for his new leg to choose this moment, this damn moment to just not. It stretched out in front of him while his other leg, his proper leg, kept trying to straighten up all by itself.

I look like a sodding Russian dancer, he thought, grabbing his gun and using that to get upright and to try to hobble-drag his way away from the Skandis, which was observing him, almost curious.

What am I missing? Ram thought.

Then he noticed the Combat Chamber had changed. It was no longer a stunning recreation of an alien world. It had reset to a plain white box. But something was different, something was wrong.

It fell into place. In the training levels the Skandis had been indistinct, with overcompressed edges. Now it was clear. Completely clear.

Ram's brain worked through three things – the forcefield failing, the rock wall vanishing, and now the chamber turning off. 'You're real, aren't you?' he shouted at it. 'Somehow you've reversed whatever this chamber does and you've come here.'

The Skandis' only reply was a nasty howl. Then it sprang towards him.

Charlie was cleaning another Combat Chamber. Automated processes took care of most of it but what was left behind were some pretty stubborn stains.

He'd noticed that most of what was left behind was human.

He wondered how the Skandis were doing? Were they winning this war?

Which was when one appeared in the Combat Chamber behind him.

The same thing was happening in Combat Chambers across the Void. Virtual environments were gradually crashing, resetting to their base states, but with the aliens still in them. And more powerful, more vicious than ever. Safe words weren't working, the emergency shutdowns weren't activating. Worse, the doors to the chambers weren't opening.

Trapped soldiers started pounding on the doors to the Combat Chambers, until the entire Bay echoed.

Then the screaming began.

Miss Quill took the change in circumstances in her stride.

'A dozen of you. Nowhere to hide. And I'm silhouetted beautifully against the walls. Lovely.'

She was firing as she spoke.

Ram was using his gun to hold himself up. If he tried to fire with it, he'd fall over.

He tried to work out a sensible solution, realised there wasn't one, and, in a moment of blind panic, whipped the gun up, and fired repeatedly as he fell back over.

The Skandis carried on leaping towards him, its body tearing apart under the blasts from his gun.

It landed on him, and promptly fell apart into three charred lumps.

In the last moment before it shattered, something very strange happened to it. Ram, eyes screwed shut, screaming, almost didn't notice it. Then he didn't believe what he'd seen. He was just stunned to find himself still alive.

Ram lay there for a while, disgusted, then slowly, with endless patience, crawled out from under the smouldering corpse.

A simple malfunction, he told himself. Nothing to be worried about. These things happen.

Damn, his leg still wasn't working.

He eyed up the door. Not great, but he reckoned he could crawl towards it easily enough. Raise help.

He abandoned his gun and started crawling towards the door. No harm done. Soon be back up and fighting. Not a great day, not the worst.

Then the air in front of him fizzed and glowed and six more Skandis appeared.

'You have got to be kidding,' breathed Ram. Then remembered he'd left his gun behind.

DO YOU KNOW ENOUGH ABOUT DIMENSIONAL COMPENSATORS TO SAVE THIS BOY'S LIFE? (SPOILER: YOU DON'T)

'What the hell is going on?' Seraphin yelled as the alarms went off.

April hadn't got a clue and was trying to tell him this, but the noise just wouldn't stop.

Seraphin was clicking in frustration at his computer. It flashed up the spinny wheel of give-me-a-minute and did nothing else.

He pointed over to what looked like a fuse box by the bathroom. April ran to it. It wouldn't open.

'Screwdriver?'

Seraphin dashed back to his desk, grabbed a penny, and used it to turn the latch. The cupboard sprang open.

Inside was a lot of complicated alien technology. And a large trip switch. She yanked it.

The alarms stopped. The room went dark.

'Don't let go of the switch!' Seraphin was yelling.

'Already have,' April yelled back, a little deafened.

'What?'

'Never mind.' April fumbled and patted her way through the cupboard, worried that at any moment she'd turn into a human candle. She found a switch, and, holding her breath, pulled it.

The lights came back on.

'Was that the right thing?' she asked.

'Yep,' said Seraphin.

'What is all this?' She pointed to the equipment in the rest of the cupboard – a series of glowing cables and pulsing arrays.

He shrugged. 'Stuff I'm not supposed to touch.'

'Ever touched it?'

'Nope,' he shook his head. 'I once totalled a laptop after I forgot to wash peanut butter off my hands when I upgraded the RAM. That stuff is way out of my league. You any idea?'

April pretended to study it very hard for ten seconds. 'No,' she announced, trying to convey in her voice that, if it had just been last year's model, then she'd have been all over it. 'What I can say is that the lights were all green, and now they're all red.'

'Gotcha.' Seraphin ran a hand through his hair. 'That's getting a bit technical for me.'

He darted over to his main computer, which had now finished starting up again. He logged in, waited, opened a browser, and then waited some more.

'Here,' he said, pointing to a display map. 'Looks like something's going on with the Combat Chambers.' He zoomed into the map. 'Got it. They're all full and the doors are offline.'

'What?' said April. 'Do something!'

'Pfft,' Seraphin jabbed at the screen. 'All I can do is see the status report. Helps me with my bulletins. I can't open the doors. Seriously. Why would you give me that power?'

'Good point.' April wasn't really listening to him anymore. 'I've got to find someone who can help us get control. And she's not going to like it.'

Ram made it to the door and pressed it. It should have triggered the opening cycle. Nothing happened. He peered through the small window, hammered on it, shouted for help that wasn't coming. Then he groaned and felt around for the manual trigger.

'Manual trigger,' he thought. What was wrong with having a door handle? This whole place was so screwed up. He located the trigger. He'd been told that the reason the doors took so long to open was in order to balance the dimensions in the Void. It was important that you didn't bring anything back from the battlefront with you. A very bit like divers having to decompress. There'd been a lecture on the possibility of bacteria crossing the dimensional barriers. It took ten seconds to fully harmonise the dimensions. But the manual trigger could do it, just about, in five. If he could find it. If it was still alive five seconds after he'd found it.

Trying to find a hidden lever while keeping an eye on six creatures intent on killing you is difficult. You know the expression about 'doing it with one arm tied behind your back'? Try doing it with only one leg. Ram had settled into an awkward crouch, his useless leg splayed out in front of him and constantly trying to tell him that it really wasn't happy. Every now and then he'd loose off a shot at the Skandis, but his gun was now little better than a water pistol.

At each blast, they'd pause, shudder, then press on. Judging from their roaring and twitching and the way their tentacles snapped, they were angry. Angry and hungry.

Only April could feel sorry for these things, he thought. He fired off a couple more shots, bought himself some time, then got back to running his hand up the door seal.

In training it had been easy. But then that was always the way with safety demonstrations. Flight attendants made it look like escaping a crashing plane was a calm saunter from fitting your oxygen mask to collecting your life jacket and nimbly stepping out into the water. But come on, it was going to be screaming chaos, wasn't it? When they'd gone on that school trip to Italy, just boarding the plane had been a fight, an actual fight, between vicious old ladies and a football team. Imagine the horror of trying to get off a plane, a plane that had just crashed. And apparently it all came down to the simple act of releasing the emergency exit doors and stepping out. Like that was going to work.

Ram found the trigger. It was, of course, just out of reach. He levered himself up as far as he could, and, fingers clammy with sweat, gripped the trigger and pulled it. So long as he kept hauling on it, it should release the door. He supported himself on his one good leg and waited.

5.

The Skandis were whipping towards him.

4.

His leg was hurting. His whole body was shaking.

3.

Their tentacles snapped at him, their horrific jaws hissing and howling.

2.

Oh, his leg hurt so much. Five seconds? Surely? Come on.

1.

A tentacle whipped past his face, spattering him with stinging slime. Come on!

0.

The door sprang open and Ram realised his mistake.

Charlie was running. There was nothing else he could do. He was in a Combat Chamber with a very hostile alien and all he had was a bucket. He'd already thrown the water out of the bucket.

A tentacle sent him flying.

Charlie lay on the ground, fighting for his breath as the Skandis came towards him.

'I'm an alien prince,' he told the creature. 'I'm not boasting, I'm not expecting any special treatment, I'm just saying this isn't how life was supposed to be.'

A tentacle threw him across the floor.

Charlie picked himself up, eyes wandering for a moment to the white wall. The whiteness was flickering, a little gentle corner-of-the-eye pulsing.

'As an alien prince,' he laughed, falling breathlessly onto his back, 'I should, right now, be leading an army.'

The Skandis stood over him, surveying him, the tentacles quivering with hostile interest.

'I don't have an army.' Charlie was still laughing. 'But I don't suppose you'd pass me my bucket, would you?'

The Skandis sprung at him, but Charlie had already rolled out of his way, and was up and running.

'I've been learning a few things about being human,' he shouted as he ran. 'And one of them is that it's a really bad idea to kill me. You see,' he paused for breath, a defiant smile on his face, 'my boyfriend is Polish.'

Charlie bolted for the door.

'Whuh?'

Tanya was exhausted and really, really didn't know why April was standing in her doorway.

'I was sleeping.'

'Tanya, I've come to ask you a favour,' said April. 'Something bad's happening and I really really could do with your help.'

Tanya blinked and yawned helplessly. 'I'm so tired,' she whined. 'Kill-me tired. There is literally nothing you could do to make me take part in whatever it is you're up to.' She narrowed her eyes suspiciously. 'Is it a peace rally? Or a folk festival? That's it, isn't it?'

April smiled. 'And that's why I brought along my secret weapon.'

Seraphin stepped into the room. 'Hi Tanya. Lovely to meet you.'

Tanya immediately grabbed her bedsheet. 'Oh dear god.'

Quill stared at the door. The manual trigger was jammed. She hammered at it with her gun. And then, having worked through a few other options, she shrugged and shot the door.

Ram lay on the floor of the Bay, listening to the frantic hammering from the other Combat Chambers. He could see a face pressed up against a window, pleading for help.

Then the face was whisked away and something green smashed across the window. There were three thumps and then nothing.

Bloody hell.

And he'd left his door open.

Ram grabbed hold of a wall and levered himself up. He had to close the door behind him. Had to. Before they got out. That had been their plan all along. He leaned against the wall, steadied himself against a door, and got ready to launch himself at his open door. He just needed a bit more strength, a tiny bit more strength ...

The door he was balanced against blew open, knocking him to the floor.

Miss Quill stepped over him.

'Nap time, Singh?' she sneered.

Stunned by the blast, and just generally stunned, Ram looked up at her. 'Close the doors!' he yelled. 'We've got to close the doors!'

Miss Quill blinked, bemused.

'Close the doors!' Ram screamed again.

Miss Quill shook her head. 'The blast,' she explained, shouting a bit. 'Bit deafened.'

Ram gestured at the doors, throwing himself forward to try and grab one.

Miss Quill stared at him quizzically.

Ram howled in frustration.

Then the first of the Skandis slithered out.

'Oh,' said Miss Quill. Finally she understood. 'We've been invaded. Interesting.'

HE CHOSE THE WRONG DAY
TO BEG FOR HIS LIFE

'I need you to look at this,' said April.

Tanya did not appear to be listening.

'This is your flat?' she said to Seraphin, amazed.

'Yeah,' he said. 'Well, it's a set, but you get the idea. Would you like me to switch my dog on for you?'

He leaned down, pushed a button, and Captain Pugsley materialised, and began pottering around the laminate flooring.

'Wow,' said Tanya. She'd been saying wow a lot suddenly, and April was getting a bit disturbed.

'Are you okay?'

'Yeah,' Tanya muttered without seeming to hear.

Seraphin winked at April, and went to stand a little bit too close to Tanya. 'Hi,' he said, and his smile went up to 11. 'Apparently you're good with computers.'

'Um,' said Tanya.

Seraphin tapped his desktop into life. 'Just … this one … here … I need someone to have a look at it.' He ran a hand slowly through his hair and shook it out. God, thought April, that is so obvious. But it worked.

'Sure.' Tanya walked over and sat down at the computer. She started pecking at it. 'What do you want?'

'People are trapped in the Combat Chambers and we need you to get them out,' Seraphin said.

Tanya squinted at the screen. 'And you want me to try and use their intranet as a way into the main systems?' She shrugged and hit view source on the page. 'Oh, easy. I have no idea who coded this page but they clearly never expected anyone with any knowledge to ever see it. No offence.' There followed a furious bout of typing. 'There. See?'

A small Java box popped up with a prompt.

'Well, that's hopeful,' Tanya remarked. 'Hardly worth you turning on the full charm was it?'

'I wasn't,' protested Seraphin. 'Back rub?'

Tanya was embedded in the system. 'It's like this was coded by aliens,' she muttered, then shrugged. 'Probably was.'

'Um,' said Seraphin, 'I was asking—'

'About a *back rub*,' muttered Tanya. 'I have no idea if that works for you, but that's just weird. Now, please just stand about half a metre in front of the screen and look vaguely hot, and that'll be fine. Okay?'

'Erm, okay.'

Tanya turned to April and smiled at her. April smiled back. And a holographic pug nuzzled around their legs.

The Skandis poured into the Combat Bay. At first it was just the ones from Quill and Ram's chambers. Then they started to open the other doors.

A Combat Chamber flew open.

A relieved soldier staggered out, only to realise what was waiting for him on the other side. A tentacle snatched him up, and threw him screaming against the far wall. The Skandis moved on to the next door.

Ram stood frozen. About an hour ago, this had all been easy – running around in a shooting gallery blasting aliens. The weirdness of the last few days had finally made some sort of sense. And now that had all gone so wrong. The surging force of Skandis – a dozen of them? – looked absurdly too big for the Combat Bay, the air already stifling with their disgusting smell. Life had got all too much. Again.

'They're invading! Do something!' Ram shouted at Miss Quill. If you're out of your depth, find a responsible alien.

But Miss Quill, either still deaf or not caring, was backing out of the Bay, firing.

'We've got to stop them!' Ram shouted louder.

'Already shooting them,' Quill snapped back. 'What more do you want?'

The Skandis crawled across the Bay, advancing as Quill retreated. Ram, edging back against the wall, kept his balance as best as he could.

Against the chaos, the screams and the blasts, he could hear a voice.

What? He twisted slightly to see what the fuss was.

Pressed up against the other side of a Combat Chamber door was Charlie. Desperate.

'Interesting.' Tanya had stopped staring at the screen and was instead looking at the holographic pug.

Seraphin knelt down and nuzzled its ears. 'Is my dog annoying you?' he asked.

'No,' Tanya's voice was subdued. 'It's just ... It's awesome.'

'It is kind of,' said Seraphin, watching as the pug clip-clopped over the floor. 'Some kind of amazing alien thing.'

'Yeah,' Tanya said. 'Sorry, distracted for a bit.' She tapped the screen. 'The systems I can get into are the helmet cameras.' She opened up a browser tab. 'We can

see everything. And there's a whole load of settings here ...'
She pointed at a series of buttons at the bottom. 'They're
greyed out, so you can't alter them, but it may be a back way
in. But to what, I don't know.'

Seraphin leaned over her, a little too close, a little too
smiling. 'Just do what you can,' he said.

'Sure,' Tanya said, and looked at the fake pug snuffling
curiously around April's legs.

Ram turned to Quill, waving at her across the Bay.

'It's Charlie! He's trapped in a Combat Chamber!'

Oblivious, Quill carried on backing away, firing.

Ram turned back to Charlie. 'We're getting you help!'
He waved his arms at Quill again.

'Miss Quill! Come here! Help me open this door!'

Miss Quill didn't seem to notice.

Charlie hammered on the door, shouting through it,
urgent, strong. 'Quill! My life is in danger! I order you to
help me!'

Quill, a world away, calmly carried on firing at the
creatures.

Ram, desperate, flung himself into the path of her gun.
Wonderfully, at the last moment, his new leg steadied him,
more or less, and he stood, wobbling, eyes shut as Quill's
bullets blasted around him.

She stopped firing. Had she stopped because he was in her way, or because the genome-lock on the gun had kicked in? Deciding he'd rather not know, he took a deep breath and opened his eyes.

'Hi,' he smiled.

'Mr Singh, what are you doing?' she asked. 'You're getting in the way of my fun.'

'It's Charlie!' shouted Ram, indicating the Combat Chamber door with a frantic pantomime.

Miss Quill followed his gesture. She rolled her eyes. 'Riiiight,' she said, with the enthusiasm of someone who has to scrape something off her shoe.

Ignoring the Skandis, she strode across the Bay, and activated the release trigger for Charlie's door.

She counted off five seconds on her fingers then threw open the door, yanked Charlie out, fired three times into the creature rushing out behind him, and slammed the door shut.

'I'm so sorry, I didn't hear you,' she said flatly, then strode away, raising her gun and shooting into the advancing horde.

April leaned over Tanya's shoulder, peering at the screen.

'Amazing,' said Tanya. She didn't stop typing. 'Honestly, endless amounts of processing power dealing with the helmet video feeds, nothing, nothing at all about opening doors or letting me help anyone. I can see the systems, I just can't reach them. It's like I'm stuck in a fish tank in a vast library trying to work out how to reach the books.'

'Yes,' said April. 'Look, I was wondering. Wondering about the Skandis and the helmet cameras ...'

'And the pug?' asked Tanya, grinning.

'Oh, you're there too, aren't you?' April laughed.

'Oh yes,' Tanya nodded. 'I do listen to what you say. Everyone's like all "We just have to fight them because they look so awful ..." and you're all flower child and "I think we should hug them" and we're all "Oh that's disgusting". But what if you're right ...'

April tapped the screen, at all the footage from the helmet cameras. 'What if I am?' she mused.

'Well,' said Tanya, 'once I can get out of my fish tank, I'll see if we can do something clever for you.'

She got on with typing.

Charlie stood, slumped and winded against the wall, taking in the situation. Monsters. Screaming. Quill with a gun and a smile. Then, gathering himself together, he went over to Ram.

'Sorry about that. She's deafened by the blasts,' Ram said, wondering why he was making feeble excuses for her.

'Sure,' said Charlie. 'You okay?'

'Yeah.'

'Good. Thank you,' Charlie nodded, and suddenly Ram saw the alien prince in him. He wasn't just reacting to the situation around him. He was considering it. 'So. We're being invaded?'

'Yeah.'

'Right,' Charlie nodded, looking vaguely affronted.

'Fancy ordering them to stop?' suggested Ram.

Charlie ignored the jibe. 'Quill said she couldn't hear me?'

'Yeah,' said Ram.

Charlie nodded again, a sad little nod that made it quite clear he didn't believe a word of it. Then he looked away, surveying the chaos in the Bay with the aloofness of a general.

Soldiers were fleeing from the Combat Chambers. There were now about two dozen creatures. The only person trying to hold them back was Quill.

'Hum,' said Charlie. Then he indicated the fleeing soldiers. 'Quill can't hold the invaders back on her own. Can you get them to help?'

'Why me?' Ram hated it when Charlie treated him like this.

'Because you're a good soldier and they respect you.' Charlie didn't seem fazed. 'It will save time.' He looked around again. 'I'm going to try and get into the systems. Maybe there's a way to block the Combat Bay off.' He turned to go. Then he stopped. He looked at Ram.

'Oh, I'm sorry,' he said, 'I'd forgotten about your leg.'

Ram blushed, feeling humiliated. But also Charlie was right. His artificial leg had frozen, rooting him to the spot.

'Here,' Charlie said, reached out his arm, and balancing Ram, led him over to the other soldiers.

'You lot,' Ram shouted at the soldiers, 'don't move – listen to me …'

Tanya hadn't stopped typing for several minutes.

'How we doing?' asked April.

'Well,' Tanya groaned. 'The fact that I'm still bashing this keyboard and not doing cartwheels should tell you that it's not good. This system was just designed to display information, not to give me control. It's maddening – I can select footage from the helmet cameras, I just can't open or close doors. I can't do anything.'

Seraphin appeared next to her, and handed her a carton of juice. 'You might not be able to do anything, but I can,' he said, and grabbed a microphone.

An alarm sounded across the Void, echoing through its corridors. The soldiers all scrambled to the Big White

Room, where footage was projected over the walls, showing the carnage taking place. Seraphin's voice boomed over it.

'So, this is happening,' he said. 'We're being invaded and we need to stop it. The best place to defend is the Big White Room. Get guns, get there, and get ready to fight. We're trying to seal off the corridors, but I doubt it's going to work.' He stopped, then started again. 'I mean, we're hoping that we'll get it to work. But we've got to do everything we can to stop them.'

At the end of the Combat Bay, protected by the rest of the invaders, two Skandis gathered around a service hatch, and, prising it open with their mandibles, began to work among the machinery with surprising skill and dexterity. An interface screen popped up, and a tentacle swiped across it, leaving a sticky trail.

'Oh,' said Tanya, 'someone else is in the system.'

'Is that good?' asked April.

Tanya squinted at the screen. 'No. Probably not.'

The soldiers had retreated to the Big White Room. There'd been nothing else they could do. The screens around them were still showing the chaos.

A fleeting glimpse of a frightened soldier, sat on a bench, despondent, no longer a soldier, not much more than a child.

Another soldier backing away as the jaws of a Skandis wrapped around her head.

A group of soldiers looking at each other, their faces blank, empty, exhausted.

Quill firing and firing and firing and laughing.

ABNORMAL. ABNORMAL. ABNORMAL.

They'd formed a barricade of sorts, using the tables and benches and a lot of hasty shoving. The Skandis, dozens and dozens of them were coming, but it had seemed the right thing to do.

'Keeping out the monsters, keeping out the night,' Charlie said, grabbing the other end of a table from Ram and shoving it.

They stood, surveying their work.

'They're coming,' someone said, and someone else stifled a sob.

With a roar, the barricade shattered, falling like a Jenga tower as the Skandis surged through.

Ram and Charlie were pushed aside. There were screams and shouts, then a soldier ran forward to confront the Skandis as they poured into the White Room.

For a moment the girl stood there. She was scared, you could see that. But she was also determined. She held her gun up, but she did not fire. Her posture, everything about her said that she was going to defend this room to the death.

A boy crawled out from under a table, and went to stand beside her. He raised his gun as well.

Three more soldiers formed a line with them.

All of them stood, pointing their guns at the rows of Skandis.

The invaders stood silently, watching them, as if curious.

The girl nodded to the rest of the line, and they all levelled their guns and pulled the triggers.

Nothing happened.

They pressed them again.

Nothing.

They turned to each other.

Then they turned back to face the Skandis. The soldiers' faces were open in a look of comic alarm, almost embarrassment. 'Well, this is awkward ...'

'Shoot them!' screamed Quill. 'What's wrong with you? Shoot them!'

But no one paid her any attention. They were staring at the five soldiers, standing there, against an alien army, just five lonely, defenceless children, lowering their useless guns in utter, miserable defeat.

The Big White Room fell silent, the walls filling with pictures – everyone was staring at the five students, alone in the middle of the room.

Ram leaned forward to help, providing covering fire from his gun, but it didn't work either.

'What the hell?' he asked.

Charlie shook his head. 'They've interfered with the genome-locking. The guns are useless now.'

Charlie was wrong.

The Skandis pushed the five soldiers back against a wall. One of them picked up a gun, examined it, and aimed it.

'No,' shouted Ram. 'No!'

But they fired anyway.

THE SKANDIS WAR AS YOU'VE
NEVER SEEN IT BEFORE

'How's it going?' asked April. 'Surely we're there!'

Tanya grunted something.

April leaned over to see what she was doing. She was immersed in a series of protocols. 'What is that?'

'Something new,' Tanya grunted. 'The Skandis have disabled the weapons. I've got to reactivate them. Otherwise it's going to be a massacre. It's all very well trying to get into the helmet cam systems, but I can't see how it's going to save lives.'

'If I'm right,' said April, 'then we won't need guns. Please. Sort it.'

Tanya shook her head. 'People are dying right now. I've got to stop it.'

April put her hand on Tanya's shoulder, but she brushed it off.

Seraphin appeared at April's side. 'I'm not her,' he said quietly, 'but there's another terminal by my bed. Perhaps we can do something there.'

The Skandis surged forward, lashing out with their tentacles. Soldiers were crouched behind whatever cover they could find, aiming their guns fruitlessly. They may as well have been yelling 'Pow! Pow! Pow!' Children playing with toys. Damn, thought Ram, that's what we've been all along. Bang bang, you're dead.

Tanya appeared on the screen, hovering over the slaughter. 'I'm trying to get the guns back online!' she yelled.

'Try harder,' Miss Quill roared back.

'Not encouraging, Miss,' Tanya said.

Benches and tables flew past, swept aside as the Skandis surged into the hall.

'Wow, that escalated quickly.' Seraphin was watching as the Skandis took control of the Big White Room. He and April sat on the edge of his bed, trying to get sense out of his tablet.

'Are you getting anywhere?' she asked.

He smiled at her, and his sweet smile was very sad. 'No, not a clue.' He tossed the tablet to one side, and

Captain Pugsley made a leap for it and vanished through the bed.

'What were you looking for anyway?' Seraphin asked, opening a drawer, dusting off an old laptop and plugging it in.

April stared at the weird half-a-dog embedded in the bed.

'Not certain. Not really my area.' April looked sheepish. 'Not really a hacker.'

'Neither am I!' called Tanya. 'What you trying to get into?'

'The helmet cam systems.'

'It's pointless. You just can't hack into them,' explained Tanya. 'Believe me I've tried. Gah,' she waved at the desktop. 'Seeing the feeds is easy, getting beyond that is a nightmare. The operating system I'm trying to talk to is weird. Like an onion skin. You peel off layers of icons to get to what you want. See?'

On screen she was pulling away sheet after sheet of icons, all of them labelled in an alien language. 'The deeper I go the harder it gets to understand.'

Seraphin had finally booted up his old laptop, and had got into the helmet camera feeds. 'We can do just as much from here,' he said. 'The problem is, it's not got as fast a processor, it'll be sluggish.'

April had one of those beautiful quiet moments where the entire world and her urge to scream at it just faded gently away.

Helmet cameras.

A slow laptop.

A holographic pug.

Empty cartons of juice.

Got it.

'You say you still get sent freebies?' she asked Seraphin.

'Yeah,' he said. 'Don't know how the post works, but—'

'Not important,' April said. 'Anything electrical?'

The Skandis swept towards the humans. People had stopped trying to make a run for it. Any attempts were met with lethal stuff. Bodies crashed and snapped against the walls.

'Stand still!' ordered Quill. 'Don't be idiots. Don't run.'

The great walls lit up, fizzing.

'Tanya!' shouted Ram. 'Is that you doing this?'

'No!' replied her voice. She sounded lost, desperate.

Washing into focus on the screen were hundreds of images of the terrified humans, lined up against a wall.

Charlie realised they were now being shown what the Skandis saw. They would be able to watch themselves being devoured.

* * *

April was tearing apart Seraphin's cupboard.

'Anything electrical?' she'd said. 'Computer stuff.'

He'd started throwing boxes at her. 'It's pretty much all useless,' he said. 'The WiFi link back to Earth from here is so slow ...'

'Good,' said April.

'And they tell me they'd rather not have stuff installed on their systems.'

'Excellent,' she laughed, pulling out armfuls of things – USB mini fans, motion sensitive Christmas tree lights, small drones, wireless dongles, thumbsticks and hard drives.

In her head, her suddenly clear, pin-sharp head she was thinking: 'What if it's not just me who finds computers annoying?' And she was smiling. She remembered how much trouble she'd had when she'd first plugged her piano keyboard into her computer.

Tanya looked up from her keyboard to see April marching through the room with a bundle of kit. 'What the hell are you doing?' she asked.

'Being very dumb indeed,' April told her. She threw the bundle onto the bed, and Seraphin began plugging them into the USB hubs.

* * *

The humans were stood in a line, waiting to die, watching themselves on the screens of the Big White Room. Some were still holding their useless guns. Others had let them drop to the floor.

'This is sick,' said Ram.

'It's an impressive act,' purred Miss Quill.

The Skandis had stopped. They were waiting. Enjoying the moment.

'Nearly there!' called Tanya's voice over the speakers. 'I've nearly got the guns back on line.'

'We. Are. Out. Of. Time,' grated Quill.

She raised her gun. All the other soldiers raised theirs.

'I would very much like to go out fighting,' Quill said. 'If that's not too much to ask.'

Seraphin scratched his head and looked helplessly at April. 'What happens now? I've plugged everything in.' He pointed at the forest of cables snaking out from this laptop across the duvet. The head of Captain Pugsley appeared through the duvet and nipped ineffectually at them.

'We wait,' said April. 'We wait for something ordinary and human to happen.'

* * *

'I'm in!' shouted Tanya. 'I'm into the weapons. They're rebooting now! Get ready to fire!'

A window on Seraphin's laptop popped up. 'New technology detected. Finding driver.'

And then another one appeared over it.

And another.

Quill and the others tightened their fingers on the triggers. They were ready to fight.

And then the Skandis did something remarkable.

THEY THOUGHT THEY'D WON UNTIL THEY FOUND OUT THEY'D LOST

'Stop!' yelled April. 'Stop! Something's happened! Can't you see what's happened?'

But no one was firing. Everyone was staring.

'What the hell?' gasped Ram.

'Oh god.' Tanya stared at her screen and gaped.

The Skandis had changed. They were no longer nightmares of tentacles, slime and spikes. They were instead so beautiful that to look at them stole a breath. They were childlike, fluttering creatures, an agreeable merger between angels and butterflies – they glowed with beauty, from their silver hair to the furthest tips of their silk wings. They hovered just off the ground, and that seemed right, as though to actually touch the floor would have somehow lessened them.

'Their faces,' gasped Tanya. Their faces were remarkable. They had about them an aura of universal beauty. Their eyes were wide and golden, they had tiny furred noses, and their mouths were delicate wispy things, their skin stretched with fine markings that suggested these were mouths made for smiling.

They were not smiling now.

April's plan had been simple. Seraphin's laptop had been crammed full of USB technology, all of it searching desperately for a new driver. The sudden inrush of requests for software, the old processor, the sluggish internet speed, all allied to do what Tanya's skills couldn't – they hit the helmet camera systems and brought them down.

Suddenly the Skandis were revealed.

'That,' said April, 'is what they really look like.'

'But—' said Seraphin and stopped. That was pretty much all anyone said. The same expression echoed down in the White Room – one of horror and disbelief. Someone was crying.

'What have we done?' Ram said.

The Skandis showed them.

The screens of the White Room lit up with footage. A thousand deaths, each one seen from the victim's point of view. Tiny hands and paws flailing up, pleading and squeaking, falling backwards, their last view the sneering faces of their killers – human soldiers, young faces twisted with rage and hate.

Once those thousand deaths had finished, they saw a thousand more, and a thousand more after that. The deaths were broadcast on every wall, the floor, the ceiling. There was no escape from them. The blasts, the screams, the laughter.

'Stop it!' screamed Tanya. 'Stop it!'

The picture changed. For a moment it was mercifully blank.

The Skandis stood, surveying the cowed soldiers placidly.

Then Seraphin's voice came over the speakers. It was missing its normal exuberance. 'We've got … we've got the other side of the picture. You have got to see it.'

He and April played out footage from the soldiers' helmet cameras. Suddenly they saw all their battles as they really had been. Where before they'd been marching through desolate wastelands, they were now marching through fields, villages, schools.

Rows of the fluttering aliens were mown down as they tended crops. Horrified parents watched as their children exploded in flame and then fought back desperately, angrily. Villagers rushed forward to try and protect their elders while urging others to flee.

The most horrible thing was how beautiful the aliens looked even as they died, flames racing along their wings, agony exquisitely expressed on their faces.

The humans watched the screens. They couldn't turn away from what they saw. The slaughter. The terrible laughter. The jokes. A rifle smashing down and crunching over and over again as a boy's voice chuckled. 'One down, three to go.' Then he turned to three Skandis children clinging to a corner.

It took a long time to play all the footage.

It stopped. Eventually.

Seraphin appeared, leaning into the screens.

He looked about to speak, and then shook his head, turned away, and the screens of the White Room went blank.

There was silence. Shock. Wonder.

Then came a thud.

Then another.

The sound of helmets being taken off. Dropped to the ground. People blinking at the Skandis. Seeing them as they truly were.

NORMAL/ABNORMAL didn't matter anymore.

Soldiers looked at the Skandis, and then they looked at each other for the first time. And realised how young everyone was.

Then the disbelief started. What if this was an illusion too? What if what they'd originally seen was true? And this was the illusion.

A debate began to rage. Shouting.

All the while the Skandis stood there, fluttering gently. Waiting.

April walked into the White Room. She walked between the two sides. Everyone watched her. She walked patiently, with poise and clarity. In that moment, Charlie couldn't help but think how grown-up she was. Ram just blinked. How could she be so cool? After all, this was *April*.

She stopped before the fluttering crowd of aliens, and bowed her head.

'I've never got to say this before, but,' and she smiled, a beautiful, sad smile. 'On behalf of the human race, I am sorry.'

There was no simple resolution. No happy ending.

It would be nice to say the aliens bowed back, and then left in peace.

They did not.

But nor did they slaughter everyone. Instead they ransacked the base, going through every file, making copies, pulling information out onto the screens, analysing it.

As far as the humans were concerned, they ignored them completely. Some people tried repeating April's apology, trying to make it personal, but it was as though they weren't speaking at all. Now that they'd made the humans aware, the Skandis had dismissed them. It just seemed easier for them to ignore their murderers. We are, April thought, beneath contempt.

Ram and Tanya sat on the remains of a bench, watching the Skandis flutter around, moving in beautiful, graceful loops as they dismantled the walls, stripping out vast chunks of technology. Tanya blinked and turned away, in case she cried again.

'I can't believe it,' she kept saying.

Ram nodded. His head kept going round and round and round. How many had he killed? How many were adults? As if that made it any better. It did not make it any better. None of it made it any better.

'I've lost count,' he said, empty. 'I keep trying to count. Oh god. I can't remember.'

'I know how many I killed,' said Tanya, very sadly. She wouldn't say.

'And, all that bants while I was doing it. Like I was a hero.'

'Yeah,' she said. 'I was laughing. Sometimes I couldn't stop laughing because I thought I was doing good.'

'We were,' he said, disgusted with himself. 'We really thought we were. And we all dared each other on.'

'It was … ' Tanya's face twisted up with shame. 'So much fun.'

'Yeah,' Ram turned away from her. 'And I finally found something I was good at.'

They sat in silence after that.

There was an angry huddle in a corner. One kid, from Coal Hill, was shaking a fist. 'Yeah but,' he was saying, 'how do we know they're still not planning on invading the Earth? I mean. They still could. Couldn't they?'

The huddle nodded. Making it okay. Making it possible to live with themselves.

If the Skandis heard, they didn't pay any attention. They no longer cared.

Seraphin appeared on a wall. Only one was still working. He was wearing black. He'd shaved.

'Hey everyone,' he said, the confidence gone, his voice croaking. 'Here's what we know,' he said. 'I think it's important we all know.' He swallowed and stopped for a bit. 'I'm getting it together.'

April moved through the crowd and sat next to Ram.

'I'm sorry,' he said to her.

'Yeah,' she said. 'You're only apologising to me because you can't make it right with the Skandis.'

'No,' he said, flushing with anger. 'You deserve an apology too. I didn't listen to you.'

'Maybe,' April said, considering. 'Maybe I'd just make a terrible soldier.'

She took his hand, and squeezed it very gently.

On the screen Seraphin stopped rifling through his notebook and then spoke again.

'The Skandis helped me understand as much about this as they could. Looks like we will never know who organised this,' he began. 'Some of you have spoken about that feeling of being watched, out of the corner of your eye. That's all we have of the people behind this. A vague idea. They made sure they were never seen.

'Can I make it clear – the Skandis were never planning on invading the Earth. They're a peaceful, beautiful race. As you've seen, their home planet is pretty amazing. So amazing that other people wanted to live there. But they didn't want to be seen being involved in wiping the rightful owners out. They approached mercenaries, but no one wanted the job.

'Instead, they came up with a plan. They found a way to Earth, and they found a way of recruiting people who could be blamed. There are not many people on Skandis – wiping them out wouldn't take that much effort. But, if we'd succeeded, the shame would have been all on us. On the Earth.

'The people behind this wouldn't just have got the Skandis world, they'd have got the Earth as well. If they'd wanted to invade us, no one would have stepped in to stop them. They're ruthless and they're clever. They've made this all our fault.

'I cheered you on. I told you to do it.' He stopped, and took a long drink of water. 'I made you do it. You made each other do it. But we'd been fooled. The helmet cams were filtering what we saw, making us see what our kidnappers wanted us to see. Massive perception filters. Nothing has been real. Every image you've seen has been altered to make you the hero of the movie of your own life. We thought we were Han Solo blowing up the Death Star. Really, we're Stormtroopers.'

He leaned back in his chair. 'One more thing. You may be wondering how they paid for all this – turns out there's still money in space. It costs to build this base, to place it in the Void, and to interface with the Skandis' home world. It cost a lot to filter the helmet cams and to buy the drugs they put in your food. Oh yeah. They drugged you. Sorry.

'Anyway, cash. Turns out, there was a site. Pay-per-view. All across the universe, people have been paying to watch what we've done. It's sick. But it's been really popular.

'The sickest thing of all? All right.' Seraphin stood up and paced the room, jamming his hands in his pockets and looking wretched. 'The people behind this. Our masters? They may not have won any planets. But they've still made a massive profit from the videos.

'Yeah, we think the universe is full of evil UFOs with probes, or of great shining space gods. Turns out, it's full of really twisted people. And not only are they The Worst, but now the universe has seen all these videos, what do you think they think of us?' He shook his head and stared bleakly ahead. 'I dunno,' he ran his hand through his hair, 'I just dunno. Perhaps we deserve whatever's coming.'

He turned. 'Anyway, whoever's running this? They've left us here to rot. The Skandis have opened the Combat Chambers up for us. We don't deserve it, but there you go. I guess they don't want our deaths on their conscience. I'm using one to go home. Maybe you should do the same. If you see me, don't say hello.' He breathed out, a shuddering breath that emptied his lungs. 'Well, that's it. Seraphin out. Mic drop gif.'

He walked away.

The great screens in the Big White Room went blank and never showed anything again.

Everyone was silent, stunned. Except for Miss Quill, who looked up, smiling slightly.

'Well, I think that was a pretty great plan.'

TO GET YOUR FREE CONFESSION JUST FOLLOW THESE SIMPLE STEPS

Miss Quill went back to her room and tapped on the wall.

'I know that you can still hear me. I know that you're still there.'

Nothing answered her.

She put her hands on her hips.

'I'm a very patient woman,' she told the wall. 'Some day soon I'm going to be the last survivor of my planet. While I'm waiting for that, I may as well hang around waiting for you to show yourselves. Time's slow here. And I'm really rather calm.'

There was no answer.

Quill carried on staring at the wall.

An hour passed. Maybe two.

'I'm still here,' said Miss Quill. 'And not at all bored. I've waited for thirty teenagers to come up with thirty different feeble excuses for not being able to solve Fermat's Last Theorem as homework. So bear that in mind. I'd appreciate an explanation from you.'

The wall looked back at her blankly.

'Here's the thing,' said Miss Quill. 'I know you're still here. The Skandis may be as dainty as dancing Disney teacups, but they're formidable transdimensional engineers. Nothing gets in or out of here without their say so, and, according to the logs, no one's tried to go anywhere other than Earth. I'd say you figured you'd stay behind. See if there was a chance to recoup a bit more of your investment.'

The wall said nothing.

'I know I'm not mad. I know you're in the walls,' said Quill. 'I knew you came out to observe me when I was resting. I am a very light sleeper, and it amused me to work out who you were.'

Perhaps it was a trick of the light, but the wall seemed to frown.

'We've met before, you see,' Quill said. 'I'm Quill. The last of the Quill. You came and offered your services to us. Said you'd help us with the Rhodians. We said no. I won't bore you with talk about a warrior's honour. You just wanted too much money. We were a poor people so we left it at that. But I was always curious about how your service worked. And now I know. Very clever.'

She smiled at the wall. The wall lit up, just a little.

'You have no name,' Quill smiled. 'The humans will find that a shame. They really do like their closure. If there's one thing they love more than an apology it's someone to hold responsible for everything wrong with their lives. And it's much easier to blame people with names. But that's not how you work, is it? You hide in the shadows, you skulk in the walls, you buy and sell planets – and no one knows it's you, because no one knows who you are. And no one ever will.'

The wall shrugged, as much as a wall could.

'It's the humans I feel sorry for,' said Quill. 'Actually, that's my first thought when I wake up every morning. But in this case, the humans will process it so badly. Their brains are so strange, so slow and fragile. Some will forget completely, some will deny it ever happened – but they'll all remember eventually, somehow. They'll all be changed by this forever. And, because they're up against you, they'll never even have a name to curse for their nightmares.'

The wall considered what she said.

'Luckily, I am Quill,' said Miss Quill. 'And we don't need names.' She raised her gun and pointed it at the wall. She fired into the wall, draining the powerpacks.

The wall shattered like a shell. Six bodies fell out, lying twitching on the ground, smoke rising from them.

'You shouldn't have hid behind the wall,' she smiled at them. 'You should have come out and faced me. The genome-lock doesn't stop me from shooting walls.'

She turned one of the charred corpses over. Its face was an empty, featureless mask.

'No names? No faces?' she tutted. 'The humans are really going to hate you.'

She turned around and went home.

HAPPY ENDINGS DON'T KILL
PEOPLE – GUNS DO

When you've caught the world out in a great lie, it takes a while before you trust it again.

For Ram it was as simple as putting one foot in front of the other.

He was running. Down the road. Into the park, round the trees and off to school.

His artificial leg kept telling him that something, it wasn't sure what, wasn't quite right.

'No,' he said to his leg. 'It isn't. Get over it.'

And, for this morning, his leg did.

Charlie slunk out of the kitchen, two bowls of cereal balanced in his hands. Miss Quill was walking in.

'You've been avoiding me,' she said. As always she wasn't angry. She was, at best, mildly amused. As though it was a childish reaction.

Charlie refused to rise to it. 'Yes,' he said, angling his chin up at her defiantly. 'Is there any reason why I shouldn't?'

She stepped past him, enjoying his slight flinch as she got close to him. She filled the kettle and flicked it on to boil, pulling a mug from the cupboard. It had a jolly puppy on it. She dropped the mug in the bin and picked another one.

'I fought. And I enjoyed it. I am honest about that,' she smiled at Charlie. 'One day, if you really hold true to your heritage, you too will fight a great war. And you will be lying to yourself if you don't enjoy it.' She tipped boiling water into the mug. 'You'll see. Enjoy your cereal.'

Tanya sneaked into the living room. The rest of the house was a hive of people, running into the bathroom, arguing over clothes and making too much noise in the kitchen. No one noticed her go up to the television and switch it on. She slipped headphones on and plugged them in.

For days now she'd made a public protest about how she was overgaming. About how she was giving it a rest. And she'd stick to it. In public, at least.

She booted up the games console.

Yes. She'd stick to it. But just a quick bout every now and then. With a smile, she started shooting.

April was standing waiting at the school gates, watching Ram approach.

'I'm all sweaty,' said Ram.

'Yeah, and you're making a thing of it.'

'Not.'

'Are.'

They stood there, a silence forming between them that wasn't quite the comfortable silence between old friends, but maybe one day would be.

Pupils were streaming through the school gates, checking their phones, laughing, nudging each other. Every now and then, one of them would catch April or Ram's eye and look away. It was the telltale giveaway.

Ram snorted. 'People forget so quickly.'

'You think?' April leaned back against the railings. 'They were abducted, tricked into being butchers – not really sure that even Coal Hill's counsellor can cope with that. And what do you say when you get home? "Sorry I've been missing for a couple of days, actually been fighting an alien war for months"? Or do you go with—'

'"Staying over at Kevin's working on a Maths Project"? Yeah,' Ram laughed uneasily. 'It's like no time's passed at all.'

More people strolled past them. A girl stopped. She stared at them, burst into tears and ran away.

'Who was that?' Ram asked.

'Not a clue,' April said. 'All those helmets.'

'Yeah.'

The sun shone, and more people slouched through the gates.

'Maybe they're all forgetting,' April said. 'There's a chance that it's only us who remember.'

'That'd be kind,' Ram agreed. 'But then, I'm no longer sure the world is that kind.'

'No.'

'But that's Coal Hill,' said Ram. 'So much to ignore, to deal with silently.'

'How long do you think we'll be able to cope?'

Ram shrugged.

April watched a kid kicking a ball around the playground. No one joined in. 'Who'd kidnap kids and do that to them?'

'Charlie says Miss Quill knows more than she's letting on, like who's behind it.' Ram sounded like he didn't really trust either of them. 'But is that … I mean, does it matter? Like I doubt we can sue them. Or that they'd even notice.'

April looked again at the playground. 'It's changed, you know,' she said. 'It's more subdued.' A sad echo chimed in her head, of her dad after he'd been drinking. 'Notice, they're all being more cautious.'

'I guess,' Ram conceded. 'I keep checking Facebook, but I'm not posting anything on it. No one really is – everyone's being …'

'Really, really cautious,' April said. 'No bragging, no videos, no food. It's like a go-slow.'

'Will no one think of the cats?' Ram asked, and they smiled at each other.

'Not so bad.'

'Not really, no. Guess not.'

They stood in silence, watching the playground. They got ready to head in, to start another day, one that would no doubt start off innocently enough and end in death and aliens.

Anyway, that was today, and it hadn't started yet.

A kid on a mountain bike whipped past them, did a stunt swerve, then another, and, at the last minute, bumped up against the curve. The bike balanced there on one wheel, just for a moment.

A dozen phones whipped up, all eager to catch the moment as the bike slowly arced backwards, crashing to the ground, landing on the rider, who rolled groaning around in the gravel. No one helped him, they just filmed.

'Too good to last,' said April.

'Yeah,' agreed Ram.

They went and started today.